CHAPTER ONE

L ADY AURORA SINCLAIR stared out at the wide sweep of lawn before her, populated by some of London's most attractive gentlemen all hovering about the early blooming primroses. She took a sip of her tepid lemonade, searching for a place to discreetly dispose of it. Like most of her family, Aurora had a taste for Irish whiskey and didn't care for lemonade, though she did like gardens.

She'd had a garden. No roses, of course. Mostly cabbage.

Glancing about, Aurora was unsurprised to see she was once more alone and unchaperoned. Not unusual. Her chaperone, Miss Charlotte Maplehurst, wasn't terribly good at her job. Aurora covered her mouth with one gloved hand, trying to stifle a bored yawn.

Is this it, then?

When first arriving in London shortly after her brother, Jordan, became Earl of Emerson, Aurora had been thrilled. Overcome. Nearly giddy with excitement after spending a decade in banishment at the broken-down estate that was Dunnings. Emerson House boasted a full larder, something Aurora hadn't seen in years. Upon her arrival, Aurora was measured for and received an entire new wardrobe. Finally, she was in the possession of dresses that hadn't been patched so often they looked like a quilt. Gloves. Bonnets. Slippers. Fans. Oh, and *books*. Dozens and dozens. Aurora was allowed to buy as many tomes as she liked from Tate's, the bookseller she favored.

Tamsin, overprotective older sister, had determined Aurora *must* have a proper debut. Live the life as an earl's daughter, the one denied her for so long. Dancing, deportment, lessons in French—which Aurora still did not speak passably well—history, riding, lessons on the piano.

Oh, she was terrible at the piano. A tragedy, really, since young ladies were often measured by such a talent.

Each lesson received was guaranteed to mold Aurora into the very epitome of English womanhood. It was the culmination of her every girlish dream, especially since cost was no longer an issue. The Sinclair family was no longer impoverished.

Dunnings, that terrible barren place where she and her siblings had been banished by their older half-brother, Bentley—now thankfully deceased—was a place one *survived*. The crumbling estate was more punishment than home. Bentley had wanted the reminder of Father's second family far from London and reduced to living on his nonexistent charity. When Mama fell ill, Bentley hadn't even sent them enough coin to find her a proper physician. She'd died at Dunnings: Aurora's lovely, scandalous mother, never once saying a bad word toward Bentley.

A true villain to the story of the Sinclairs, Bentley had been abetted in his actions by his horrid maternal aunt, Lady Longwood. What a terrible human being her half-brother had been.

Aurora didn't miss him in the least.

She hoped Bentley spun about in his grave knowing that while he'd left the earldom mired in bankruptcy due to his poor management and lavish spending, his hated half-siblings were now obscenely wealthy. *Coal* had been found at Dunnings. Not just enough to light a warm fire if the night grew chilled, mind you, but *buckets* of coal. Dunnings was now considered one of the largest coal deposits in all of England. Ironic, given the Sinclairs had struggled for years to make the ground at Dunnings produce something other than cabbage.

None of them had anticipated coal.

SINFULLY WANTON

The Five Deadly Sins
Book 5

Kathleen Ayers

ARE YOU SIGNED UP FOR DRAGONBLADE'S BLOG?

You'll get the latest news and information on exclusive giveaways, exclusive excerpts, coming releases, sales, free books, cover reveals and more.

Check out our complete list of authors, too!

No spam, no junk. That's a promise!

Sign Up Here

www.dragonbladepublishing.com

Dearest Reader;

Thank you for your support of a small press. At Dragonblade Publishing, we strive to bring you the highest quality Historical Romance from some of the best authors in the business. Without your support, there is no 'us', so we sincerely hope you adore these stories and find some new favorite authors along the way.

Happy Reading!

CEO, Dragonblade Publishing

Additional Dragonblade books by Author Kathleen Ayers

The Five Deadly Sins Series
Sinfully Wed (Book 1)
Sinfully Tempted (Book 2)
Sinfully Mine (Book 3)
Sinfully Yours (Book 4)
Sinfully Wanton (Book 5)

The Arrogant Earls Series
Forgetting the Earl (Book 1)
Chasing the Earl (Book 2)
Enticing the Earl (Book 3)
The Haunting of Rose Abbey (Novella)

Aurora discreetly tipped over her glass of lemonade into the potted fern beside her and wandered closer to a servant holding a tray of what appeared to be champagne. She really shouldn't. Champagne wasn't her spirit of choice. Neither was the ratafia some of the ladies were indulging in. But, she reasoned, giving a roll of her shoulders, one must make do.

The champagne was delightful. Refreshing. Much better than the lemonade, though she would have preferred whiskey. She finished the bubbly, pale pink liquid in moments. Another glass was in order.

She snatched one without being noticed.

Staring out at the colorful display of gowns and cheerful attire surrounding her, Aurora considered how she'd once longed to be part of the social whirl. Dreamt of being a lady and dancing in a handsome gentleman's arms. Her debut was made in a stunning confection of pale rose decorated with brilliants. A tiny tiara had been woven into her dark curls and diamonds dangled from her ears, a gift from Tamsin. Aurora's first dance had even been with a duke. Her brother-in-law, Ware.

She swished the champagne around in her mouth, stopping only to take a small tart from yet another servant's tray. In truth, there was little else to do.

London had shuddered at the news that the brazen, wanton, rides-astride, Lady Tamsin Sinclair had wed the Duke of Ware. Seduction, the gossips claimed, was to blame for poor Ware's downfall. Tamsin the Temptress.

In truth, the seduction had been nonexistent, at first, and most of the fuss caused by a moth. Tamsin and Ware were madly in love, as ill-matched as they might seem at first glance.

Good lord. Aurora looked down to find her glass already empty again. She'd have only one glass more, though her tolerance for spirits was much higher than the typical young lady. Given she was a Sinclair.

A typical young lady.

Aurora snorted. No one had warned her how dreadfully dull

her second Season would be after the initial excitement of her first. Boring. Yawn inducing. Nothing of import to discuss but gowns, horses, and the weather.

She placed her empty glass on a nearby table, twirled about and quickly slipped herself more champagne from the refreshment table without a soul noticing. Raising the fan dangling from her wrist, Aurora waved in annoyance at the thin sheen of sweat coating her chest and cheeks. The small burst of air provided was welcome but not nearly enough. The tent was tightly packed, overly warm, and had the press of too many bodies.

One staunch matron, overly plump, and clad in lavender with a spray of violets stuck in her coiffure, sent a disapproving look, her gaze lowering to the half-empty glass of champagne clutched in Aurora's hand. Her companions did the same, assessing Aurora, all reeking of judgmental propriety.

Aurora deliberately brought the glass to her lips and swallowed the remainder of the champagne.

She tilted her chin mulishly, ignoring the gasp of shock at her behavior, having become accustomed to such censure. Lifting her skirts, Aurora sauntered in the opposite direction, careful not to drop the empty glass. Well, what did it matter? Most of London was waiting patiently for Aurora to prove to be a *Deadly Sin* despite her perfect behavior, affected modesty, and connection to a duke.

Aurora tried to take a deep breath and found she couldn't. Discarded her empty glass for more champagne, all while tugging at the bodice of her gown which was far too tight but eminently fashionable.

A young lady's clothing was no more than a snare made of silk, meant to trap her beneath mounds of petticoats, lace, and cotton. Aurora hadn't thought, when dreaming of the marvelous future awaiting her, that so many bloody clothes would be required. Tamsin, who was far more generously curved, often lamented that corsets had been invented for the sole purpose of torturing a woman into silence. One could hardly breathe, let alone speak or enjoy a good meal, if laced too tightly. Corsets, Tamsin claimed, were nothing more than a conspiracy visited upon all womanhood.

At the moment, Aurora had to agree. She toasted her new-found understanding with yet another glass of ... something. Not champagne this time. A punch of some sort. She didn't even recall finishing her last glass.

As she sipped, her eyes fell on a profusion of shrubbery to the right of the tent, festooned with ribbon and set some distance away. A hedge maze. A rather decent sized one. Two topiaries stood guard before the entrance. Lions, Aurora thought, tilting her chin. Or possibly rabbits. From this angle it was really impossible to determine. While she detested her wasted afternoon at this garden party, the maze intrigued her.

Why didn't something happen?

A drunk lord bursting into a bawdy tune. A couple caught taking liberties with each other behind a tree. Anything to relieve the boredom of this party. At the very least, more of this delicious punch should be circulated.

No sign yet of Miss Maplehurst's trim form and cloud of silver hair. How bloody difficult could it be to find one slight, elderly woman dressed in a shocking shade of puce?

As it turned out, impossible.

Miss Maplehurst, or Aunt Lottie, as she liked to be addressed, wasn't much of a chaperone. Nor was she Aurora's aunt. Charlotte Maplehurst was the much older, spinster relation of Jordan's wife and countess, Odessa. She'd once served as her niece's chaperone with mixed results, but after Odessa wed Jordan, Aunt Lottie generously offered to help guide Tamsin and Aurora into society.

Guide being a charitable term.

Tamsin and Ware had ruined each other in Lady Curchon's garden under Aunt Lottie's watch.

But the older woman, because of her neglect, was *perfect* for Aurora. Aunt Lottie did not hover or chastise, at least not much, and she was quite progressive in her views. Despite her age, she never missed an opportunity to discreetly ogle a handsome gentleman, often pointing out a muscled backside or demanding breadth of shoulders to Aurora. She'd unashamedly eyed each of Aurora's brothers as if they were the last biscuit on a tea tray.

Given her nature, Aunt Lottie did not object to Aurora enjoying a stolen kiss or two when the situation was warranted, reasoning that her charge should have a bit of fun but also reminding Aurora that while her budding sexual curiosity was natural, she must be careful not to go too far. Rules were in place for a reason. A ruined reputation would possibly result in a marriage not necessarily to Aurora's liking and add yet another scandal to the Sinclair family.

Aunt Lottie came by her knowledge firsthand. A spinster by choice, she'd had her fair share of adventures with gentlemen and still did. Leaving Aurora on her own at a garden party in pursuit of her own pleasures was not an unusual occurrence. Aunt Lottie and Aurora had a silent agreement to not mention such things to the rest of the family. Today, her chaperone had vanished after catching sight of a dapper, silver-haired gentleman leaning heavily on a cane as he made his way across the sweeping lawn. A hand had gone to Aunt Lottie's throat, eyes wide.

"Excuse me, dear," she'd murmured, and promptly hurried off. Aurora hadn't seen her since.

"Good for Aunt Lottie," she stifled a small burp behind her fan. "But it has been some time. Perhaps I should look for her."

Sidling toward one of the tent openings, Aurora cautiously made her way through the crowd, trying not to trip into anyone. The ground in the tent was not accommodating for slippers in the least. Quite uneven. She nodded politely to two girls who she'd become acquainted with during her debut. Both had later joined Aurora for a stilted afternoon of tea and gossip presided over by the Dowager Duchess of Ware. She suspected their invitation had more to do with currying the favor of Ware's mother than it did with Aurora.

Just as well. Neither was the least interesting. She couldn't even recall their names.

No matter that the dowager duchess had sponsored her, or that Aurora's come-out ball had been held at Ware's extravagant London mansion. The smiles and applause had only been for her first Season and practically nonexistent in her second. Oh, she still received plenty of invitations, after all, no one in London wanted to anger Ware's formidable mother. But Aurora had no real friends in society.

She was still a *Deadly Sin*.

So, what if her mother had once been an actress and Father's mistress before becoming Lady Emerson? The only person who still thought that particular scandal relevant, one over two decades old, was the detestable Lady Longwood. Horrid, bitter woman, hater of all things Sinclair, Lady Longwood circled Aurora at every opportunity, waiting breathlessly for a misstep. Praying for Aurora to be reckless and ruin herself.

She sighed and helped herself to more punch. Nearly as bad as the lemonade. The rum could barely be tasted.

Ruination wasn't completely out of the question. Aurora had a curious, inquisitive nature which was bound to get her into trouble. At times, she worried she might be wanton. She thought a great deal about physical relations.

Whistles and loud laughter erupted from the game of bowls on the other side of the lawn. Perhaps Aurora would head in that direction. Bowls had to be more exciting than wandering around this tent with no one to talk to.

"Lady Aurora," the raspy tenor sounded from just behind her.

She stopped abruptly, allowing the sound of the man at her back to ripple deliciously across her arms and chest while bathing in the enticing aroma that always hovered about his shoulders. Something light with a touch of citrus mixed with leather. Heat bloomed from the center of her chest to cup her breasts.

Goodness. The punch had made her overly warm.

Aurora turned, cheeky, brazen smile pasted on her lips, one

she'd practiced before a mirror for just such an occasion.

"Worth."

The beautiful man before her bowed, giving Aurora a lovely view of his gilded locks, tousled about his head.

There was absolutely no denying the charm of Charles Worthington. It came as naturally to him as breathing. Her brother Drew's best friend and business partner was an entirely decadent temptation, like one of the elegant, three-tiered cakes she'd seen in the window at Gunter's. All sculpted to perfection, with only enough adornment to draw the eye but not detract from his looks. She'd once heard the Dowager Duchess of Ware equate Worth to an angel, but one who possessed the reputation of a devil.

Aurora looked up at him, taking in the fit of a perfectly tailored coat, cut in an exacting manner to the lean, graceful build. Even having been in his presence dozens of times, Mr. Charles Worthington still had the sort of masculine magnificence that shocked a woman near senseless.

Honestly, Aurora needed a moment to compose herself.

"I didn't expect you to be here, Worth."

Sapphire blue orbs glittered back at her, snapping to the glass of punch she held. "Where is Miss Maplehurst?"

She peered at him over the glass of punch, deliberately taking a large sip, pretending to savor the taste, before deciding to answer.

"You haven't seen me in months and that is the first thing you can say?" How disappointing. "I believe she is seeing to her own affairs." Aurora had an unwelcome fixation on Worth, compounded by not just his looks but also by the friendship they'd once shared.

Before she came out.

Worth leaned in and sniffed. "I can't tell if you are foxed or not."

"Not," Aurora assured him, though she was likely headed in that direction. "I was raised on good Irish whiskey, if you'll recall.

I have an exceptionally high tolerance for spirits. This," she held up the punch, "is merely watered-down lemonade."

A dubious look crossed his handsome features.

Aurora breathed him in. Like nearly every other female in London, she was taken with Charles Worthington. How could you not be? She found him to be experienced, probably in ways she shouldn't know about. Handsome. A bit of a rake, but not *too* terrible. He didn't go about debauching young ladies, for instance. Intelligent. Sharp-witted.

Pity he often treated Aurora as though she were a child in pigtails.

"I'm surprised you are in attendance," she said, ignoring the way the skin along her arms prickled at his nearness. "I haven't seen you at any of the events I've been to in months." Her gaze dipped to his mouth. Nicely shaped lips. Sensual curve.

Amusement flickered in his eyes at her assessment. "I received an invitation to this lovely party and I like gardens, quite a bit, as it happens. Bees. Honey. Peonies and roses. I don't spend all my time on business matters."

Untrue. Her brother often said Worth was one of the most determined, hard-working individuals he'd ever met. A trait Worth shared with Drew's wife, Hester.

The citrus aroma became more pronounced as he drew closer. There was a tiny, nearly invisible dot of something purple at the corner of his mouth. Wine, she thought. The tip of her tongue darted out to wet her upper lip.

I want to lick that bit of wine.

Worth took a step back, cocking his head. "Why don't I find Miss Maplehurst for you?" His gaze had grown shuttered. His tone, more formal. As if he'd guessed at Aurora's thoughts and meant to put some distance between them.

"As I said, I believe she is otherwise occupied."

"I think it might be best if you return home." Worth sounded so very staid. Taking the glass of punch from her hand, he said, "Let us find your chaperone and I'll see you both to your carriage."

Annoyance.

That was the other strong emotion Aurora felt in Worth's presence. Treating her as if she were some jam-covered child who he was duty-bound to supervise. "Isn't there a widow or two about who requires your attention?"

"Possibly, but I'll see to you first."

"Kind, but unnecessary. I'm considering if I should join a game of bowls—" She gestured to the other side of the lawn. "Looks amusing enough."

"You're terrible at bowls, Aurora. You nearly took my foot off the last time we played."

"A one-time occurrence." Truthfully, she had little athleticism in her, unlike Tamsin, who could ride better than most men and play a decent game of bowls. Try as she might, Aurora couldn't seem to toss a bowl correctly, and she *had* nearly taken Worth's leg off. He'd hobbled about for the remainder of that afternoon in an overly dramatic fashion, requesting Aurora fetch him a glass of brandy. Or a cheroot. She'd even had to bring a pillow for him to prop up his ankle.

Yes, but that was before.

"The incident you speak of was some time ago, Worth. Besides, Lord Grisham has offered to teach me." She gave a shrug. "I'll be in his capable hands." Gazing at him from beneath her lashes Aurora couldn't resist adding, "Your tutelage leaves much to be desired."

"I was a fine teacher. You declined to heed my lessons."

Aurora had been far too aware of Worth's attention to her that day to pay attention to any lessons on bowls he might have given her. She'd blushed and stammered, glancing at her feet to avoid looking at Worth, which was skin to lifting one's eyes to the sun.

"That is a matter of opinion," she replied.

"I fear Grisham wishes to educate you in other matters." A wrinkle marred his perfect brow. "I'll escort you to the lawn while we search for Miss Maplehurst."

"You'll do no such thing. But if you are that concerned, you could offer to teach me yourself, Worth," she said in a bold tone, no longer speaking of bowls. There had been many times, given her attraction to Worth, when Aurora imagined the two of them trapped in a torrid embrace.

The beautifully sculpted features tightened into a stone mask. "Aurora."

"Ugh," she waved him away. "I already have three brothers. I do not require a fourth." Aurora was beginning to regret she'd ever set eyes on Charles Worthington, especially today. There was once a time when she couldn't wait for his arrival at Emerson House. He came often to dine with the Sinclairs, and after, everyone would gather to play cards in the drawing room. Worth would often partner her, explaining the fine points of whist. Tell her amusing stories. Talk to her of books. He was exceptionally well read.

But after her debut, Worth no longer made a point of calling at Emerson House. When he did dine with the family now, which was rare, he avoided Aurora. There was no more partnering him in whist. Or sharing a jest together.

The evening of her debut, Worth stood beside Aurora, casting witty observations at the swirling mass of guests to keep her nervousness at bay. He'd loomed nearby as each gentleman approached, far more interested in Aurora's dancing partners than her brothers. Worth fetched her lemonade and a plate of tiny cakes. Charmed the dowager duchess. Joked with the rest of her family and drank a great deal of wine with Drew.

And Aurora had basked in his attention, waiting for him to bow and lead her out on the ballroom floor.

She was sorely disappointed.

Worth partnered with a half-dozen other ladies in attendance, including Tamsin, who stepped on his toes and couldn't carry a tune to save her life.

But Worth did not dance with Aurora.

She'd worried over that, later. Cried a bit as she went to bed. If nothing else, Aurora assumed Worth was her friend. But after that night, he behaved quite differently toward her, when before he'd—

"Come. You can't go wandering about on your own, nor approach Grisham in your state." Worth gave an exasperated sigh, as if she were a problem he needed to solve. His entire manner had Aurora's blood boiling. He didn't even offer Aurora his arm to escort her to Grisham. Unsurprising given Worth had not taken her hand in greeting since before her debut. Not once, in her recollection of that evening, had Worth even so much as brushed against her skirts. As if she were suddenly diseased. At first, Aurora's fingers would hover stupidly in the air while waiting for him to take them, but now she didn't bother.

She looked down at those long, graceful fingers. Two twitched, drumming along the edge of one muscled thigh. He probably made good use of those sensual digits, taking elbows, and kissing a lady's knuckles, but never hers.

Which was perfectly fine. Honestly.

Aurora shrugged off the pinch. And Worth.

"Lovely to see you, Mr. Worthington," she uttered in a polite tone, sailing away before he could say another word. Aurora swung her hips gently as she walked, hoping he might stop her.

But Worth did not follow.

CHAPTER TWO

A SHORT TIME later, Aurora, still smarting from her encounter with Worth, found Lord Grisham as well as another glass of punch. This cup was far stronger than that being served in the tent, probably due to the number of gentlemen playing bowls. She fanned herself while watching Grisham stride across the lawn, admiring his backside as he flung his bowl with accuracy. The young earl was terribly attractive. Well-mannered. Athletic. The exact sort of gentleman whose attentions Aurora should encourage.

Regardless of Worth's unwanted opinion.

Aurora took another sip of her punch. Grisham *was* appealing. Didn't treat her like an infant *and* she'd caught him staring at her mouth. Grisham had potential.

She waved at Grisham and he immediately came to her side, greeting Aurora with a smile and asked if she cared to partner him in the next match. Aurora declined, regretfully of course, mindful of her terrible skill at the game and the fact she'd had enough punch now to make her more than a little clumsy. Also, she had no real skill at bowls. Even so, Grisham smiled at the fleeting touch of apology she gave his arm.

Sipping at her punch, Aurora entertained herself by watching Grisham stride about. She was determined to put Charles Worthington and her own childish fantasies concerning him out of her mind. It was clear to Aurora that in the months since the last time she'd seen Worth, nothing had changed. Her last encounter with him before today had been just before Worth had gone to Lincolnshire to visit Drew and Hester. Worth had called at Emerson House to inquire if Jordan wished to send a letter to Drew, not bothering to hide his disappointment that Aurora had been the only one at home.

He hadn't even asked after my health.

Nor did he stay for tea. After pacing about the drawing room for some moments, Worth had bowed and taken his leave.

Aurora swallowed another mouthful of the punch, blinking as the game of bowls went out of focus. There was a light, euphoric sensation making her mind buzz about, making it difficult to concentrate. She pulled her attention back to Lord Grisham. Difficult to determine if they would suit or not, especially if he stayed gentlemanly. Aunt Lottie often said a man's passionate nature, or lack of one, could be determined with a kiss or two.

Unfortunate then, that a young lady could not ask a man to kiss her. Not without an uproar.

Aurora was of the opinion that a kiss, or even allowing a discreet liberty, would go a long way in deciding whether a gentleman suited her. She knew of far too many young ladies who had ended up wed to a gentleman they hadn't yet kissed. How on earth could you enjoy what Aunt Lottie termed, *bed sport*, if you didn't even like him kissing you? Revulsion was soon to follow along with a miserable state of affairs.

Aurora swished the last bit of punch between her teeth. She was quite resolute that not be her future.

Aunt Lottie had been kind enough to draw Aurora a version of a male appendage on a piece of paper one day, reasoning that someone must have the conversation with Aurora. Neither Tamsin nor Odessa had done so. Also, Aunt Lottie was growing concerned that Aurora's overt curiosity about such things might lead to ruination.

Yes, Aurora was curious, but she'd also grown up in the country. Animals *did* breed, she reminded Aunt Lottie. Jordan had kept pigs, after all. But the older woman still insisted on drawing what she deemed the male appendage on a scrap of paper. The illustration more closely resembled one of the wintered-over carrots Aurora had once pulled out of the barren earth of Dunnings. Not something she wanted—

A giggle burst out of her thinking of that carrot and comparing it to what lay beneath Grisham's trousers, for instance.

A sniff of disdain sounded from her left where the esteemed Lady Harriet sat perched on a chair, watching the game of bowls. Proper and demure to the core, parasol raised high overhead to protect the pale skin of her cheeks, Lady Harriet had probably never been kissed. Aurora doubted she knew males even possessed an appendage protruding from their bodies. If a gentleman so much as touched the sleeve of her dress, Lady Harriet might faint dead away.

"Lady Harriet." Aurora inclined her head politely, struggling to keep from giggling again. "I didn't realize you cared for bowls."

Lady Harriet's perfect lips pursed at the near-empty glass of punch in Aurora's hand. "Do you think it good manners to go about half-foxed at a garden party, Lady Aurora? I suppose that's one way of garnering the attention of a gentleman if one can't trod the stage."

Aurora didn't flinch. Slurs against her mother, a former actress, were bantered about on a regular basis. She'd heard far worse.

"Much better than surveying the world with a sour countenance I would guess." Aurora shrugged. "Doesn't all that sneering put them off?"

"Do you plan to lure Grisham into the grass and pretend to search for butterflies?"

A direct insult to Tamsin, who'd been ruined due to a moth landing on her knee, which enticed Ware. The moth, not Tamsin. Initially.

"You should be more careful," Aurora murmured, pointedly surveying Lady Harriet's forehead, which she thought overly large. "Frowning so much is sure to give you wrinkles."

Lady Harriet gasped in outrage, before burning Aurora with a look of scalding dislike.

Very well. It appeared her stay at the game of bowls was nearing an end.

She remained for at least another quarter hour, unwilling to give Lady Harriet the satisfaction of leaving too soon. Absolutely no one, outside of Lord Grisham, paid her the least bit of attention. Eventually, Aurora stood, stumbling a bit as she walked away.

What a boring party.

Waving at Grisham, Aurora decided the maze might offer more amusement.

CHAPTER THREE

CHARLES WORTHINGTON STARED at the subtle twitch of Lady Aurora's pale blue skirts as she made her way toward the lawn and Grisham, legs wobbling slightly. He should never have entered the bloody tent after seeing her inside and left her to the poor chaperonage of Miss Maplehurst. Why had he chosen to attend this ridiculous garden party? Contrary to what he'd told Aurora, Charles didn't actually adore flowering shrubs and the buzzing of insects. Lady Berriwell, their hostess, didn't even provide decent refreshments, save the punch.

The point was to avoid Aurora Sinclair, her lush head of chestnut curls, and her tempting, generous curves. Not inhale the sweet honeysuckle coming from her warm skin. Or stare at her lips. His entire body had gone taut with lust the moment he'd seen her weaving about the tent trying not to spill her punch.

Aurora was a particular sort of madness for Charles.

Charles Robert Worthington was a rake and had no intention of being anything else. Granted, he was far from the worst in London, but he'd been blessed with a physical appearance that females of every age found appealing. He never lacked for companionship. When one is merely the second son of a viscount and not the heir, you are left to pursue your hobbies or vices as the case may be. Discreet debauchery. Which he *enjoyed*.

Which was why he kept his distance from Lady Aurora Sinclair.

The urge to punch Grisham in the nose if he so much as laid a finger on Aurora was merely because Charles didn't want the sister of his best friend ruined at a garden party. The Sinclair family was only now starting to regain some standing in society, and Aurora going off and compromising herself and creating a scandal would be disastrous. Charles and Drew had business to conduct. As did Aurora's brother, Malcolm.

So, you see, it wasn't jealousy.

Emerson needed to rein in his youngest sister. Worth wasn't oblivious to her thinly veiled innuendo. Nor her curiosity on sexual matters. Today she'd been studying his mouth, scant minutes from pressing her lips to his and—

An ache wrapped around his waist and sunk between his thighs.

Damn it.

There was a valid reason he didn't venture to Emerson House. *Temptation.*

Charles had known the night of her debut, when he'd finally been forced to admit Aurora was no child, that staying as far away as possible from her was his only defense. One touch of her fingers was all it had taken. She hadn't even noticed. But Charles did. The attraction to Aurora had surged like a dozen thunderbolts up his arm. He'd spent the entire evening glaring at her dance partners. He hadn't so much as allowed her skirts to touch his legs since.

Today, just the aroma of honeysuckle, so decadent and lush, had made him wish to press Aurora into the grass and raise her skirts. Nose along the soft hair between her thighs, inhaling her essence, taste her—

He, Charles Worthington, completely undone by a girl not yet twenty.

My god, I cannot be in her presence again.

Not only would Drew never forgive him, but Aurora had two other brothers, one who used to brawl for extra coin and the other a former mercenary. Then there was Emerson's butler,

Holly, who had fists the size of hams.

Charles liked his looks and meant to keep them.

"There you are, darling." Fingers plucked at the back of his coat, sliding suggestively up his shoulder. "I've been searching everywhere."

Oh, yes. He'd forgotten she would be here.

"Well, you've found me," Charles answered, thankful for the distraction, even if it took the form of Lady Bryant.

Hildie, Lady Bryant, looked up at him with a seductive grin on lips painted a deep crimson, leaving no doubt as to why she'd sought out Charles. Hildie and he had been lovers briefly, years ago, but now only dallied when circumstances suited them both. A way to pass the time when attending the same tedious house party or other mediocre event, such as this little gathering hosted by Lady Berriwell. Their relationship was purely of a physical nature.

Charles, as a rule, didn't form romantic attachments.

Hildie pouted, arching her back so that her generous bosom nearly touched his chest, a favorite ploy of hers. She possessed little subtlety when it came to her needs. "If I didn't know better, I'd think you weren't happy to see me, Worthington."

"Perish the thought." Hildie wouldn't notice his sarcasm. She was completely self-absorbed. No wonder Lord Bryant looked elsewhere for his amusements.

"Bad boy," she cooed. "I've had to practically chase you down. Distressing to say the least. I was so pleased when I saw you traipsing about."

"I doubt I've ever done so. Traipsed, that is."

"And look," she gestured to her left, ignoring his comment, "Lady Berriwell has been kind enough to provide a maze for our use."

Two topiaries shaped like lions stood guard over a narrow path of hedges strewn with colored ribbons. The maze stretched in the opposite direction, and he couldn't make out the end, though it was unlikely to be terribly large. Charles hadn't been inside a maze since he was a child.

"Come, aren't you curious, Worthington?"

About a great many things, but not Hildie.

Her perfume floated in the air around him, heavy and overly floral. Gardenia, he thought. The scent stung his nostrils. Nor did it rouse his cock like the aroma of honeysuckle on Aurora's skin.

Yes, but you can't have her.

"Do you like games, Worthington?" Fingers clutched at his arm, as Hildie pulled him in the direction of the maze until they were hidden from sight beneath one of the larger topiaries. Ribbons of every color and tied to the hedge fluttered in the wind.

"I suppose it depends on the game, doesn't it?" he answered.

"You adore my games." Hildie stood on tiptoe, tongue darting like a tiny serpent, and licked at his bottom lip, begging Charles to kiss her.

Hildie wasn't unattractive; she was stunning, if he were being truthful. And he was only human.

"Lord Bryant won't come looking for me, he's too engrossed in a game of bowls and Lady Perse's bosom," Hildie whispered against his lips. Standing back, moving her hips seductively, Hildie unwound the scarf at her throat. She sauntered into the maze, trailing the wisp of fabric behind her. Knowing Hildie, she'd probably worn the scarf today purely to use for this purpose.

"I don't care for mazes, Hildie. On principal." He turned his head in the direction of the game of bowls. Only madness lay in that direction.

"Think of this more as a hunt, darling. I'll leave a trail for you to follow." She gave him a lascivious leer, dropped the scarf, and let it trail behind her as she sauntered into the maze. "Think of the reward when you find me."

"I'm dreadfully easy to motivate," Charles smiled, strolling leisurely after Hildie, pausing to pick up the scarf before the maze branched in two directions. A glance toward the right showed one glove artfully displayed on one hedge.

Laughter erupted on the other side of the lawn where he knew Aurora to be, but Charles firmly took a step forward.

CHAPTER FOUR

T HERE WERE AT least two entrances to the maze, Aurora mused. The one glimpsed from the tent earlier and now, one before her. There were no topiary lions guarding this entrance, only something that resembled a hedgehog.

Aurora tilted her head to observe the artful cutting of the hedge.

Or a pig.

Ribbons festooned the branches of the hedge before her, all clustered together by color. She assumed the idea was for one to take up a handful of say, red ribbon, and string the silk behind you as you went along so as not to become lost in the maze. Her hands stroked the ribbons for some time in indecision. Finally, Aurora chose blue, to match her dress, nearly falling into the branches.

"Drat." She brushed leaves and a stray twig from her sleeve, feeling only a bit unsteady. "The ground is far too uneven at Lady Berriwell's." She blew a puff of air at a chestnut curl that fell over one eye. Clutching the ribbons, Aurora made her way down the path, humming softly. A maze, at least, would provide some amusement. Grisham, though handsome, wasn't terribly entertaining.

Not like Worth.

Aurora frowned, stomping quickly down the path until she came to a juncture. Two choices, right or left.

"Hmm." She tapped a finger. "Right, I think." She tried to imagine the shape of the maze in her head, but her thoughts kept drifting back to Worth and his annoying handsomeness. Nothing at all to mar his perfection. Not so much as an ill-placed mole. Or a wart. If there was only something, Aurora might be able to put aside her—affection? Lustful tendencies? Curiosity? He'd taken his coat off when they'd played bowls so long ago. At the time, Aurora had been struck dumb by all that long-limbed elegance, thinking of having his form pressed against her own.

Heat bloomed once more, this time stroking along the skin of her stomach.

She forced the curl back once more, groaning in frustration. Placing a blue ribbon on the hedge before her, Aurora twirled, nearly lost her footing again, straightened, and continued on.

Aunt Lottie might well be hiding in the maze somewhere. Lord Kenebruke was the name of the gentleman she'd gone sprinting after. After careful questioning of Grisham during the game of bowls, he had confirmed the elderly man's identity. The Earl of Kenebruke, oddly enough, was from Northumberland, where Dunnings was located.

Life was full of coincidences.

Ribbons littered the hedges, perhaps left by some of the garden party's other guests who'd traversed this same path earlier, making it entirely possible to become confused about which blue ribbons were hers. Aurora plucked at the ribbon, glancing back the way she'd come. She hadn't been paying any attention to the number of turns she'd taken.

With a shrug, Aurora continued. Sooner or later, someone would find her missing and come looking in the maze. Maybe Grisham. Or Aunt Lottie.

Please let it be Worth.

"Drat. No," she said out loud. He was more likely to put her over his knee and spank her as one does an errant child. She imagined her skirts up, laying across his lap—the sting of his palm against—

"Oh dear." She clutched the hedge to keep from stumbling as the warmth pulsing along her stomach reached up to circle both her breasts. Those graceful fingers would touch the skin of her bare bottom. Glide over the back of her legs.

Aurora nearly fell into the hedge once more.

"You should be trying to find a way out, Aurora." Nodding, she stepped down the path again, the sound of her own voice a bit of comfort.

The maze hadn't looked terribly big when standing in the tent or viewing it from the game of bowls, but now that she might be lost inside the tall, sharply cut greenery, the maze had become enormous. And deathly quiet. She could no longer hear the musicians playing near the tent nor the shouts from those guests engaged in a game of bowls.

If worse came to worst, and she couldn't find her way out, no one came looking—she forced the vision of Worth out of her mind—Aurora could simply squeeze through the hedges. Yes, she'd likely tear her gown. Branches and thorns would pull at her hair giving the appearance she'd been up to no good and possibly cause a bit of gossip. But eventually, the lawn *would* appear. Or something more horrifying. Such as Aunt Lottie in an indelicate situation with Lord Kenebruke. That seemed far more likely.

She stopped before a topiary of a fox set at the end of this row of hedges. Her brow furrowed. Hadn't she already passed this way? The punch had muddled her a bit.

Stepping around the fox, Aurora squeezed through the hedges behind it, certain she'd come out on the lawn. But all that was before her was the gravel path and another row of hedges. She cocked one ear, listening for any sound, and heard nothing.

"Perfect. I am lost. I wish I'd thought to bring some punch with me."

She went back through the hedge to the fox once more and traced her steps. The problem became apparent immediately. There was an overabundance of blue ribbons. She'd no idea which were hers or if any of them were. She strode down the row and took another turn, only to find herself before the bloody fox once more.

"This is ridiculous." The silence was deafening. Not so much as the chirp of a bird. "Left." She tapped her chin once more. "No, right." Aurora turned and headed down a path that didn't look the least familiar. "Drat."

She spun sharply at the burst of crimson ribbon wound around one shrub, the ends batted about in the breeze. At least someone had been this way. Parts of the hedge looked as if they had been snapped.

Someone else had gotten lost and decided to go through the hedge and not around. The idea made her feel somewhat better.

Aurora eased herself inside the thick hedges, frowning when the sharp edge of one branch snagged on her skirts. There was also the problem of the stupid crimson ribbon, far longer than the ones in her hand for some unknown reason. The ribbon had somehow managed to twist around her ankle. She bent to try to untangle herself, but the sound of her skirts tearing stopped her. Good grief. Trapped in a hedge, slightly foxed and shredding her clothing.

This was a *terrible* party.

"Naughty boy, Worthington," a throaty, feminine voice made its way through the hedge.

Aurora froze. Lifting her chin ever so slightly, she caught sight of a small clearing in the maze containing a statue. A Greek god of some sort, though Aurora couldn't see clearly enough to determine which one. She was far more shocked at the sight of Lady Bryant lifting her skirts up her silk-clad legs.

Her initial reaction was to flee immediately, or at least, close her eyes.

Aurora did neither. She was far too curious and—well—this involved *Worth*.

Worth and the buxom, snotty Lady Bryant. Not the scenario Aurora would have wished, of course, but her overabundant interest in such things as well as the lovely euphoria surrounding her from the punch kept her firmly fixed inside the shrubbery. Worth *was* well known for his exploits with the fairer sex. Even her brother Drew, who had never met a widow he hadn't tupped, declared himself a puritan next to Worth.

Aurora leaned forward. She was bound to see something wicked.

"Come closer," Lady Bryant whispered, lifting the mass of her skirts even higher as she braced herself against the statue. Playfully, she rucked the fabric up to her waist, giving Worth a narrowed, seductive look.

Oh. Goodness.

Mouth popping open, Aurora could do nothing but stare. Dumbfounded. At Lady Bryant's—*lady parts.*

Heat seared Aurora's cheeks. Was that what her own *parts* looked like from that angle—

Lady Bryant lifted one knee and widened her thighs.

Aurora's gaze dropped down the length of her own skirts, trying to envision—well, she'd never really looked, had she? A mirror might help her examine—possibly when she returned home today.

"Hildie." Worth's form strolled gracefully across the grass to stand before the statue, efficiently blocking the view of Lady Bryant and her bits. His head cocked to one side as if considering the sight before him. "I'm not going to fuck you in the middle of this maze. Especially on that poorly executed statue of Zeus."

Aurora inhaled sharply hearing such—vulgarity coming from Worth's beautiful mouth. The sound of the word on his lips had her breasts tightening.

This was much better than watching the game of bowls.

"I thought it was Apollo. Come kiss me," Lady Bryant purred, whipping her skirts about, the only part of Lady Bryant Aurora could still see. Worth blocked from view everything else.

Abruptly, he kneeled before Lady Bryant.

"Will you kiss me, Worth?" Lady Bryant sounded quite out of breath, as if she'd been running about the maze instead of posing with her skirts held up at her waist. Her hand fell back to land on the statue's stomach.

Worth's fingers trailed up her silk clad legs pausing mere inches from Lady Bryant's—*lady parts.*

"Use that tongue of yours," Lady Bryant panted. "I want a kiss."

Aurora placed her palm over her mouth, jealousy erupting from her, yet she could not look away. This was a fascinating act. One Aurora was curious about. Aunt Lottie tended to ramble after a few brandies and gave vague details about a great many things. Just the idea of Worth's beautiful mouth. On her— *Aurora's*—lady bits left her unexpectedly damp between her thighs.

A tiny gasp left her.

Worth went completely still, his entire body growing taut. The elegant fingers disappeared from Lady Bryant's thighs. With one smooth movement he came to his feet, head leaning to the side as if listening for something.

He heard me.

"Worthington—" Lady Bryant almost wept with disappointment. "Please don't stop."

"I heard something."

"A squirrel," she pleaded. "Pray continue."

Worth spun around to face the hedge, hair glistening like gold in the sunlight streaming through the hedges. The blue of his eyes narrowed, focused on the exact spot in the hedge where Aurora stood.

Oh no. No. No. No.

"A bird, perhaps," Lady Bryant begged, uncaring that she still held her skirts rucked up in such a lewd manner. "This isn't even the center of the maze. Only a forgotten corner. I can get on my knees." She dropped her skirts. "You keep standing."

Aurora's eyes widened further. Lady Bryant had no shame whatsoever.

"Worthington." When he didn't answer, she stalked over to

him, her frustration evident. Trailing her fingers over his thighs, Lady Bryant wedged herself between Worth's legs. "You've always liked me on my knees. Don't you remember that dreadful house party we both attended in Suffolk. We had such fun. Take the scarf." She nodded to the scrap of silk on the ground. "Bind my hands. I won't even struggle."

"You rarely do, Hildie." Worth's gaze didn't move from the hedge. "But that isn't necessary," he replied in his usual, charming way pushing aside Lady Bryant's questing hand. "I fear," he looked up at the afternoon sun, "that the party will be ending soon. You should go back, my lady." He pulled a pair of gloves and one slipper from inside his coat, thrusting them into Lady Bryant's hands.

"But—"

Worth bestowed a brilliant smile on her, one guaranteed to make any woman's heart pause mid-beat, just as it did Aurora's. "Plead a headache and I'll see you home in my carriage." His eyes returned to the hedge. "It's a long drive back to town, isn't it? Some entertainment would be welcome. I'm going to stay a moment and have a cheroot."

Aurora silently and frantically attempted to work her skirts free of one sharp branch, but the blasted bush refused to release her. She had to get free before Worth decided to investigate.

"Very well." Lady Bryant did not appear pleased by the turn of events. "Give me a half an hour. Bryant will stay and play bowls the remainder of the afternoon. He might possibly decide to spend the night which would suit me well." Her skirts swirled about her ankles in a flurry of silk. "I'll expect you soon, darling."

The crunch of Lady Bryant's steps on the gravel of the path faded after a few moments.

Aurora waited patiently for Worth to follow his paramour— she rubbed her chest at the sting—and stayed perfectly quiet. She focused on her breathing, composing herself, and ignored the alarming way her nipples had tightened into painful peaks earlier. All from the mere thought of what Worth had meant to do to her—

Not me. Lady Bryant.

The pulse between her thighs refused to abate though Aurora had seen nothing but a half-naked Lady Bryant. But the mere suggestion had...*stimulated* her. Somewhat.

The bluest eyes Aurora had ever seen pierced through the greenery around her. "Toss yourself out, Aurora."

She swallowed and stayed silent. Perhaps Worth would assume Aurora was just a bit of silk ribbon if she didn't move.

"You realize that I can *see* you. And hear your breathing. You're the only lady at this party with a dress that shade of blue. Fortunately, Lady Bryant is nearsighted and refuses to wear spectacles due to her vanity. Lucky for you." He leaned a bit closer and sniffed. "And you smell of rum punch."

Biting her lip, she refused to move.

"Aurora." Worth took another step. "Don't make me pull you out. You're staring right at me."

"Well, this is somewhat embarrassing," she finally whispered.

"Out. Now."

"I'm not a child, Worth. No need to speak to me as one. I'm sure you assume I was following you about but I was merely trying to get out of the maze. The game of bowls grew tiresome and I wanted to explore. My coming upon you was purely accidental." She cleared her throat. "Frankly, I am horrified at your sordid behavior."

"Is that why your cheeks are flushed?"

"I'm overly warm."

"I'm sure you are." There was a bit of mockery in his tone.

"There is a ribbon caught about my ankle." She jerked her foot. "Red, if you must know."

"I don't care." Worth made a disgruntled sound but reached inside the hedge to take her arms. "Are your skirts free?"

Sensation burst over her limbs at feel of those beautiful fingers pressing into her arms. *Finally*. Worth was touching her. A sound erupted from her throat. Bliss, possibly. The same noise came from her when she bit into a custard tart.

"You really are foxed. I'm going to have a word with Miss Maplehurst."

He tugged on her arms, bracing one foot inside the hedge, working her efficiently out of the branches. Aurora stared at him, those handsome features taut with concentration, leaves batting against his aristocratic nose and chiseled jaw as he struggled to get her free.

She wanted to kiss him.

"What is it?" He paused, giving her an odd look.

"Nothing," Aurora assured him. "Only that I don't wish you to be so angry."

"Had I not seen you, would you have stayed silent and watched?" he said quietly.

"I—" Her cheeks heated again. Mortification filled her.

"Don't answer. I don't want to know." Worth tugged once more and Aurora balanced in the air for a moment, ribbon still twisted about her ankle as she tried to kick herself free before the bit of silk snapped, sending her flying into him.

He flew backward, wrapping his arms deftly around Aurora's body and twisting so that he would take most of the impact as they hit the grass.

So lovely of Worth. Truly. Considering.

He landed flat on his back with a whoosh, Aurora sprawled haphazardly atop his broad chest. "Get off, Aurora. You're heavier than you look."

"I'm not," she replied.

Worth wasn't bulky with muscle like her brothers Jordan or Malcolm, but lean and sculpted, much like the statue just a few feet away. Aurora's fingers stretched carefully across the span of his shoulders, watching the way the blue of his eyes darkened. Cool air brushed across her ankles and calves because her skirts were bunched around her legs and his.

Aurora did not slide off him.

She came up on her elbows, studying Worth. There was a

tiny bit of gray at one temple. The lines radiating from the corners of his eyes. The full, sensual lips and strong jaw, the latter dusted with bits of gold hair. He had a tiny freckle on his left cheek. How interesting. She'd never noticed the freckle before.

"Worth," she said. "I think I should kiss you."

His eyes widened in horror. "No, you absolutely should not. The rum punch has made you nonsensical. You've no idea what you're saying. Now get up."

Aurora didn't move an inch. A thick, pulsing hardness pressed up at her through the layers of fabric between them. And those lovely, delicious sensations, the tightening of her nipples along with the humming warmth coursing through her blood hadn't abated in the least.

She slowly twisted her hips, sliding deliberately over the ridge caught between her thighs, fascinated at the sounds Worth made as his eyes fluttered shut for a moment.

"Stop that," he growled. "This instant." He made another noise as if he were in pain.

"Your eyes are very blue, Worth." She tilted her head, observing him.

"I'm aware," he snapped, appearing more flustered than Aurora had ever seen him. Worth's composure never slipped. He grabbed hold of her shoulders but didn't toss her off.

She rocked against him once more, this time with more pressure.

"Dear God, please stop."

This was incredibly encouraging. Worth was unsettled. Somewhat pained. Best of all, he wasn't regarding Aurora as if she were a spoiled child. Not any longer.

"You don't know what you're doing."

"I disagree." Aurora knew exactly what she was doing. About to satisfy a great deal of her curiosity as to what it would feel like to kiss Worth. Have his arms around her as she'd often dreamt. Possibly she could encourage him to take liberties.

Aurora leaned forward and pressed her lips to his, marveling at the softness. Worth tasted of wine and the hint of a cheroot. Her tongue tentatively touched just the edge of his lip, licking gently at the edge.

"Jesus," he cursed under his breath.

"Kiss me back," she whispered, cupping his beautiful face between her hands.

"You are not yourself, Aurora. You've had champagne and rum punch. I can't even believe you were able to stumble about."

"I told you I had a high tolerance for such things. And I am not foxed," she answered brazenly, nipping at his bottom lip, sucking gently at the flesh. The butcher's son, in Spittal, had taught her that. While Jordan was inside discussing his pigs, she'd been in the alley behind the shop being kissed. That was the first time Aurora thought she might be...wanton.

"Where in god's name did you learn to do that?" The words were shaky.

"Don't you like it?"

"I didn't say that." Indecision flickered in his eyes a moment before a soft groan of resignation came from him. Worth lifted his head, fixing his mouth more firmly to hers and took control. His arms wrapped around Aurora and pulled her tightly against the hard lines of his body. A big hand cupped her bottom, caressing one plump cheek as the other cupped the back of her head.

Oh.

Aurora's mouth was taken. There was no other word for it. Previous kisses by gentlemen other than Worth had been tame. Polite. But not this expert ravaging of her lips and mouth displaying a hunger Aurora hadn't anticipated. His tongue twisted about hers, exploring every corner of her mouth with such mastery, she was soon reduced to nothing more than a bit of burning ash. A whimper came from inside her chest, entire body aching for Worth.

How lovely it would be if she could kiss Worth whenever she wished. Have him touch her. Stroke the intimate spaces of her body. Her fingers grabbed at his collar, refusing to let go.

Abruptly, Worth pulled his mouth from hers, eyeing Aurora as one does a wild animal. He sucked in a lungful of air. "I've kissed you. Now get off."

"You don't mean that."

"I do."

The hard length of him, pulsing up between her thighs, said otherwise. Aurora could well be laying atop a hot poker. Worth was aroused. By her. But he would never admit to it. Nor would he confess he wanted to keep kissing her. A real shame because Aurora thought kissing Worth to be nothing short of marvelous.

"You liked it," she challenged, feeling powerful. "Kissing me." Aurora's fingers slid up the side of Worth's neck to his chin. "Would you like to take a liberty?"

Worth turned his head and cursed a string of vile words under his breath. "You shouldn't say such things."

"I thought we were friends, Worth."

"Aurora—"

"Would you rather I kiss Grisham? Or say improper things to Atherby?" Aurora named another one of her admirers. "I haven't been able to convince Grisham to take a liberty with me yet, but I'm getting close."

"Dear God."

"I'm only curious and—"

"What must I do for you to cease this nonsense?" he said, sounding as if she were strangling him with his cravat. "You're going to end up compromised, Aurora." The blue of his eyes dropped to the curve of her mouth. "Such a scandal would hurt your family, after all Emerson has done to restore his reputation. Is that what you want?"

"Of course not." A tiny burst of guilt settled in her chest.

"I must insist you not go about propositioning the likes of Grisham or anyone else."

Well, it wasn't really up to Worth, was it? "I can't help myself," she murmured. "I could be wanton."

A sound left him. She couldn't tell if it was arousal or sheer terror at her words.

"But I've thought of a solution." Aurora leaned in and trailed her tongue along the corner of his mouth.

"Who taught you to kiss?" he hissed. "You shouldn't—"

"Unimportant," she interrupted what was sure to be another speech admonishing Aurora for her behavior. "Henceforth, you should be my teacher in such matters." Aurora felt rather proud of herself. "You're concerned for my reputation and that of my family, aren't you? But I am curious, Worth. I have questions. If I have your tutelage I wouldn't have the urge to experiment with Grisham," she reasoned.

"I am not going to ruin you."

Poor Worth. He was no match for her determination.

"Heavens, no." Aurora shook her head as if it was the most absurd idea anyone had ever had, Worth ruining her. Though honestly, he was rather perfect for the job and he was vastly experienced in pleasure.

"Are you mad? You are asking me to be your bloody tutor in," he choked. "Things of a physical nature."

"Well, why not? Who else should I go to? We are friends. You don't want a scandal to erupt around the Sinclairs, which is certain to happen if I were to approach anyone else with such a request. Grisham, for instance, would be honorable if he took liberties."

"And I wouldn't be?"

"Worth," Aurora gave a tiny laugh. "You'd be a *terrible* husband, as I'm sure we can both agree."

"I don't want to be a husband at all."

"Exactly. I'm certain you know the best ways to satisfy my curiosity without taking my virtue. Rest assured, Worth. Marriage is the last thing I want from you. I want to wed for love."

"Your observations are rather unkind. I have some honor left."

"Which is why you wouldn't ruin me, even accidentally. You'll guard my virtue far more ferociously than I will." Aurora pressed her hips down once more, satisfied when his breath hitched. The heady feeling from the rum punch was making her rather bold. "This is a brilliant solution."

"Absolutely, positively, *no*. You are out of your bloody mind."

Aurora brushed her mouth with his, eliciting a noise that assured her Worth would capitulate. Eventually. Just as she would marry for love.

Rolling to the side, Aurora came to her feet, heart racing wildly about in her chest. She brushed bits of grass and twig off her skirts, as Worth stared up at her.

"No, Aurora."

"We'll see." Calmly walking over to the hedge, she pushed herself through the branches.

CHAPTER FIVE

W HAT THE BLOODY *hell had just happened?*
Charles lay in the grass, blinking up into the sun. Had he hit his head on the bloody statue of Zeus?

"I think I've just been blackmailed."

Aurora Sinclair, brazen little minx, had just asked Charles to satisfy her inquisitive nature on sexual matters least her curiosity about such things lead to ruination and scandal, which would damage the reputation of her family further.

Because Charles would be discreet and not accidentally compromise her.

Good God.

Charles stood, brushing the grass from his coat and trousers, which were so tight they were in danger of cutting off his circulation.

"*Practice* on me? What am I? Some sort of fencing dummy? A stud put out to pasture to please the mares?" The thought of bending Aurora over, lifting her skirts, perhaps over a fence in some bucolic countryside and—

Damn. It.

He'd heard the tales of the former Lady Emerson, Aurora's mother, the same as everyone else in London. She'd been an actress, considered wanton, tempting the Earl of Emerson to make her his mistress. The scandal had quieted to a whisper until Tamsin and the Duke of Ware were found in a compromising situation which resulted in marriage. Like mother, like daughter, the gossips intoned. Now society watched for Aurora to make the same misstep and indeed be her mother's daughter.

Which Aurora was bound to do if she wasn't stopped.

A bark of laughter came from him. "This is worse than being tempted by the devil himself. How preposterous she would even assume that I would agree."

His cock twitched. Twice.

But wouldn't it be better than Grisham touching Aurora? Or some other idiot?

"I can't honestly be considering her proposal." He turned to the path and started walking back out the way he'd come. Charles didn't care for mazes, but he was rather good at puzzles and had memorized every turn he'd made fearing he'd be trapped indefinitely with Lady Bryant. All the while his mind worked out the dozens of scenarios in which he could pleasure Aurora while leaving her virtue intact. Debauched, wicked things.

His cock throbbed again.

"No." Charles stopped abruptly. "How would I ever look Drew in the eye? Or Emerson, for that matter?"

Aurora would cause a scandal of monumental proportions if her behavior didn't cease. Society would be outraged. Not even the Duke of Ware or his formidable mother would be able to salvage Aurora. As a friend of the family, wouldn't Charles be saving her from such a fate?

What utter rubbish, though he sounded noble.

The entire walk back through the maze, Charles considered and reconsidered Aurora's ridiculous proposal. Debated the merits. Chastised himself repeatedly for even entertaining the very idea. Images of Aurora, naked before him, hair falling over her breasts as she asked for direction kept flooding his mind making any sort of decision impossible.

"I am not completely honorable, but I can't go about de-bauching the younger sister of my best friend and business partner," he mused under his breath. "Though I dearly want to.

Nor can I allow her to risk her reputation."

Charles was a rake after all, which made Aurora's assumption that she would be somehow safe under his tutelage mildly insulting. But entirely true. He wouldn't risk being forced to wed should Emerson find out. The only sane thing Aurora had said was that Charles would make a terrible husband.

Marriage was not in his future. Not anymore.

What the hell was he going to do?

Charles came out on the lawn and caught a glimpse of Lady Bryant waiting just outside the refreshment tent, probably looking for him. She waved seductively in his direction.

So, no. He would *not* engage in the improper sexual tutelage of his friend's sister. But perhaps he could satisfy her curiosity in another way. Charles possessed a book, a rather wicked one, that he could give to her. There were detailed explanations. An illustration or two. The former diary of a former courtesan should be able to answer nearly all of Aurora's questions.

Charles pulled the edge of his coat more securely over his thighs. He didn't want Hildie assuming, *wrongly*, that his cock was interested in *her*. Beautiful as she was, Charles didn't have any intention of tupping her.

Lady Bryant would be disappointed at having to find another way back to town.

CHAPTER SIX

A FTER BARGING THROUGH at least three other hedge rows, Aurora finally popped out of the maze with a hole in her skirts, several curls springing about haphazardly about her temples, and a scratch along one arm. Frankly, given the way she'd thrown herself through the branches she was rather lucky the damage hadn't been worse.

Unfortunately, she had no idea exactly where she'd ended up. Another section of the lawn, perhaps? Nothing looked familiar. Lady Berriwell's garden party was much larger than Aurora had ascertained from the tent. She walked along the unknown stretch of grass to a small garden abloom with color. Tucked into a corner of the lawn, bright pink roses circled a small stone bench beneath the broad branches of an oak tree.

Another statue greeted her as Aurora came closer. A goddess with stone curls styled about her head.

Making her way to the bench, Aurora sat with a plop and spread out her skirts, sighing at the tears and snags in lovely blue gown. Her temples had started to ache and she might have broken the heel on one of her slippers.

All *Worth* it.

Literally.

What a marvelous experience. There wasn't any regret over kissing Worth. Or writhing on top of him. She'd do so again in an instant. Aurora meant to relive that small space of time repeatedly while waiting for Worth to capitulate. Tomorrow, over tea and a bit of toast, she would recall how he smelled of citrus, not lime or lemon, but a mix of both. How the stubble along his jaw had felt against her fingers. Her breasts still ached from having been pressed tightly to Worth's chest. The place between her thighs still hummed.

Oh, that kiss.

Aurora placed a hand to her forehead and considered swooning on the bench.

She'd threatened him with becoming a horrible scandal, shocking her family and all of London if he didn't give in to her demands. Which she wouldn't. Aurora would do nothing to harm her family. The Sinclairs had been through quite enough, thank you.

Plucking at her skirts, the ache in her temples throbbing, Aurora acknowledged that after trying, unsuccessfully for the better part of nearly two years, she'd finally gained Worth's attention. But he was just as likely to pretend she hadn't. Probably go back to not touching her. Which would be for the best.

If Worth agreed to her little proposal, Aurora was certain she'd leave with her virtue intact. Her heart, however, was another matter.

Worth made no secret of his disregard for marriage. He was even more disparaging concerning love and romance. One night, after dining at Emerson House, he'd proclaimed after experiencing love once, he had no desire to do so again. Romance was for poets and no one else. Marriage for those that needed to produce an heir, which thankfully he did not.

Even if Worth agreed to her outlandish proposal, Aurora would only ever have him physically, which was better than never having him at all. And if she didn't satisfy her sexual curiosity with Worth, because they were one and the same, Aurora wasn't sure she could move on to the right gentleman.

She hadn't lied. Aurora would wed for love or not at all. She refused to be the lone Sinclair who married for something as mediocre as money or status.

"If it came to it, I could merely enjoy Worth."

"Oh, I agree. Charles Worthington is a man created for women to enjoy." Aunt Lottie appeared from the other side of the topiary, eyes sparkling, grass stains on her skirt as if she'd been rolling about on the lawn, which she very likely had. "But I'm uncertain whether you should indulge."

"Unlike you?" Aurora nodded to her chaperone's gown. "I trust you reacquainted yourself with Lord Kenebruke?"

"Don't sound so put out. I only left you for a short time." Aunt Lottie blushed, which was alarming given her age and flirtatious manner.

"It has been hours." Aurora rubbed her forehead. "I may have overindulged in the rum punch."

"I assumed you'd stick with the champagne. What?" Aunt Lottie's brows raised as she took a seat beside Aurora. "You don't care for ratafia. Or lemonade."

"You are a terrible chaperone." Aurora nudged her gently. She adored Charlotte Maplehurst, even if she was somewhat negligent in her duties.

"I am sorry, dear. But Lord Kenebruke and I haven't seen each other in some time. Years, actually. There was much to say."

"Hmm."

Aunt Lottie maintained that she'd never had much decorum, not as a young lady and certainly not as an elderly spinster After three Seasons filled with questionable behavior, her father had chosen a gentleman for Aunt Lottie to wed. She'd refused, choosing to remain unwed rather enter what she deemed a disastrous arrangement.

Aurora had no idea who the gentleman in question had been—Aunt Lottie only ever referred to him as a "disgusting turnip"—but at the time her refusal, along with her behavior, created a fair amount of gossip. Since then, Aunt Lottie had had a discreet string of lovers. Of which Aurora was certain, Lord

Kenebruke had been one.

"I don't believe I've ever seen you move so quickly, Aunt Lottie. When you caught sight of Kenebruke."

"Pah. I merely strolled in his direction."

"You were sprinting as if your skirts were on fire."

"Well," Aunt Lottie winked. "They were."

Aurora took in her head of silver curls with a wry smile. Aunt Lottie was incorrigible. "You've got flower petals stuck in your hair."

"Do I?" She reached up to pluck them out. "There's a strong breeze today. I'm sure the petals blew free and settled on me. I was merely walking through the gardens with Lord Kenebruke. Sedately, I might add. He uses a cane."

Aurora glanced down at the dirt covering the hem of Aunt Lottie's skirts. "You must have come across a bit of mud."

"Lady Berriwell's flower beds are not as neatly manicured as you would imagine, Aurora. I stumbled a bit, but Kenebruke caught me. He's quite steady and strong despite the cane." She patted Aurora's hand. "I apologize for leaving you for so long. The party is quite dreadful. Boring in all the worst possible ways. I saw Lady Harriet earlier."

"None of the young ladies tolerate me, especially Lady Harriet. The only excitement I had was watching Lord Grisham play bowls," Aurora answered.

"Ah, Grisham. A nice pair of shoulders. Strong chin. But let us return to Worth."

Aurora bit her lip to keep from laughing out loud. A gentleman's name rarely passed her chaperone's lips without some sort of assessment of their person. "Lord Grisham is lovely."

"But a trifle boring," Aunt Lottie said, "Worth is not. I've always found him to be attractive and charming."

"Did you know Worth would be here?" Aurora looked at her. "I was surprised to see him here. Or at any event where I happen to be. Worth avoids me and has for some time."

"I don't think that's true."

"He no longer calls at Emerson House."

"I imagine business matters keep him quite busy. And he called at Emerson House so frequently because Drew resided there. Now Worth must travel to Lincolnshire to see him." A wistful sigh came from Aunt Lottie. "Such a gorgeous man."

"Who? Worth?"

"Well, yes, of course. Worth is magnificent. But I was thinking of Kenebruke." A glow lit her features and Aurora could clearly see the young girl she'd once been.

"How long has it been since you last saw Kenebruke?"

"Not since just before he married. Quite literally." A laugh escaped her. "The young lady he wed was sickly, even before she became his wife. London was deemed unhealthy for her, and they retired to his estate in Northumberland. He never had any children. His nephew is his heir. She's dead now. His wife."

"Grisham speaks highly of Kenebruke. How odd his estate is in Northumberland."

"Yes, but Ravensdale is on the other side of Northumberland, not near Dunnings at all. He'd never even heard of the place until recently. Because of the coal. Apparently, everyone in Northumberland is now digging up their estates." Another sigh came from Aunt Lottie, along with a great deal of melancholy. "I had no idea about—Lady Kenebruke. She's been gone for some time."

"Would you have sought him out if you'd known?" Aurora asked carefully.

Aunt Lottie looked down at her lap. "I don't know."

The older woman often alluded to her somewhat reckless past, especially after a brandy or two. She claimed dozens of men had fallen in love with her—possibly an exaggeration—but she herself had only been in love once. The gentleman in question was already wed and far too honorable to take a lover.

Could this mysterious lost love be Kenebruke?

"I look forward to meeting Lord Kenebruke when he comes to call at Emerson House."

"I have asked him to call upon me," Aunt Lottie replied. "Now, please don't tell Emerson or Odessa that I abandoned you for such a long time. Though I had good reason." She waved a hand. "I do hate disappointing your brother by neglecting my duties. He has such faith in me. Misguided though it may be. You'd think he would have realized there were limits on my abilities when he courted Odessa."

"I can assure you that your title of chaperone is merely ceremonial at this point, Aunt Lottie. I think Jordan is well aware of your faults. But my brother isn't terribly good at being an earl, so he's no room to criticize. Think of all you've accomplished. I'm halfway through my second Season and haven't been compromised. You must take your victories where you can."

"I suppose I shall. Is there anything you would like to confess to me about Worth?" Her shrewd gaze traveled over Aurora, lingering over the mess of her hair and the tear in her gown.

"Not at all."

"I adore Worth, but he has a reputation, Aurora. And a past." Her lips pursed. "I'm not sure—"

"You need not worry," Aurora assured her. "Worth is simply Worth. My brother's friend. Far too old for my tastes. If anything, I find him annoying. He treats me as if I'm a child."

"Does he? Where is it you saw Worth? The maze?"

A blush stole up Aurora's cheeks before she could stop it. "He was with Lady Bryant."

Aunt Lottie made a face. "I thought he had better taste. Well," she took Aurora's hand.

"Shall we take our leave of this dreary party? Lady Berriwell plans to have dancing on the lawn which is a terrible idea. There are holes everywhere and I've no desire to sprain my ankle. Thank goodness the appearance of Kenebruke salvaged the afternoon."

"Yes, thank goodness," Aurora mused.

As they made their way back across the lawn, her thoughts once more settled on Worth. There had been a moment, right after Aurora kissed him, that the light in his eyes shifted from annoyance at her antics to wonder. Those graceful hands had held her close without reservation.

CHAPTER SEVEN

AURORA YAWNED BEHIND her fan as discreetly as possible.

In yet another instance in which she decried the bland tediousness of a young lady's existence, Aurora had been forced to attend a recital. Recitals in general bored her to tears, specifically those musical performances hosted by a desperate mama to showcase her unwed daughter's nonexistent talent in hopes of attracting a suitor.

Aunt Lottie, in a surprising burst of chaperonage, barely left Aurora's side the entire evening. Just now, she stood by the refreshment table conducting a somewhat heated discussion with Lady Curchon, Ware's aunt. The pair didn't really like each other, especially after Lady Curchon's plan to keep Tamsin from wedding her precious nephew hadn't worked, for which she blamed Aunt Lottie.

Reluctantly turning her attention to Lady Mormont's daughter, Agnes, Aurora had a rush of pity for the poor girl dutifully plucking away at the strings of her harp. She couldn't think of anything worse than being asked to perform like a circus animal for the likes of Atherby and Mendenhall. One of them was sure to offer for Agnes. Both were in need of a dowry to replenish the family coffers.

The information of either lord's poverty wasn't well known, but Aurora's sister-in-law, Alyss, was extremely well-informed about nearly everyone in society. Surprising, since Alyss wasn't a gossip, nor did she usually attend events such as these.

A large feather bobbed at the outer edge of the small gathering, the bearer turning her sharp chin, making sure Aurora was aware of her presence.

Lady Longwood was such a predictable, detestable creature.

A slow, smug smile crossed Lady Longwood's angular features as her eyes roved over Aurora, head to toe. A knowing glance said that Aurora was just steps away from becoming the shame of London.

Vulture.

Aurora gave Lady Longwood her back and stepped closer to an alcove directly across from the line of chairs where most of the guests were seated. Bentley's maternal aunt was a vile woman. She'd never forgiven any of the Sinclairs for the insult dealt her family, making sure that when Bentley inherited, her revenge upon them all was enacted.

Dunnings.

Aurora still recalled the day of her father's funeral. Mama weeping her heart out that the man she loved was gone. Lady Longwood hadn't even given them the courtesy of allowing them to grieve, instead she'd had Bentley ship his hated half-siblings off to a remote estate. And Mama had died.

Deadly Sins. That's what you are.

"Lady Aurora, may I say you look quite fetching in that gown. Blue is my favorite color. I've brought you lemonade."

"Is it, Lord Mendenhall? I hadn't known." She accepted the lemonade. "How kind. Thank you."

Mendenhall was wasting his time on Aurora. While her dowry dwarfed that of harp-playing Agnes because coal had made the Sinclair family wealthy, Alyss had ferreted out that Mendenhall was far too careless with his coin and thus would not make a suitable husband. Which was just as well because Aurora had no real interest in Mendenhall. But she liked him well enough. She lifted her glass and took a sip.

"You are welcome." His brow wrinkled. "Perhaps I merely do

not enjoy music, but I find I'm not amenable to the harp."

"Nor I, my lord." Aurora gave a small laugh. "Perhaps if Agnes were sporting wings. Like an angel."

Mendenhall chuckled. "Do you play an instrument, Lady Aurora?"

"The piano, if you must know. I'm getting better, though I struggle." The piano was really something Aurora had wanted to master, but she found it increasingly difficult.

"Perhaps you don't have a proper teacher. I'm rather good, if I must say so." Mendenhall gave her a wink. "Started when I was five or six. My father played as well. Should you require a tutor, Lady Aurora, I most humbly volunteer."

"While I'm sure your talents are boundless, Mendenhall, Lady Aurora already has the finest tutors available." Worth appeared from behind Mendenhall, a glass of wine dangling from one hand and Lady Duggins, a blonde buxom widow, from his arm. "Don't you, Lady Aurora?"

The skin of her arms prickled softly and the smell of that light, citrus scent filled the air. Worth smelled a little bit like an orangery. He was warm, the heat coming off his body teasing along her shoulders. She was less pleased to see Lady Duggins.

Aurora shrugged. "I like to learn new things, as you well know," she said pointedly to Worth. "I think it very kind of Lord Mendenhall to offer me his expertise. I'm sure he could teach me something new." She said the last mainly to goad Worth a bit.

The room erupted in applause for poor Agnes as she finally finished. She stood and took a bow, relief lighting her features while Lady Mormont preened beside her daughter, keen eyes scanning the crowd, until finally settling on Mendenhall.

A resigned sigh came from Mendenhall.

"Excuse me, if you will. I believe Lady Mormont requests my presence." He gave a short bow. "Lady Aurora, Lady Duggins. Mr. Worthington."

As soon as he departed, Worth leaned over and sniffed at her glass of lemonade before nodding approval. "Merely checking."

Aurora nearly threw the lemonade right in his gorgeous face. "That was unnecessary."

"As is your need for a tutor," Worth bit out. "Especially if it is Mendenhall."

"Have you considered tutoring then, as I asked? I've so many questions. A boundless curiosity."

Lady Duggins looked between them. "I'd no idea you played the piano, Worthington." Her fingers plucked at his sleeve. "A gentleman of many talents."

"I quite agree, my lady," Aurora said.

Worth's features shuttered. He took a deliberate step back from Aurora. "Have you had too much punch again?"

"I'm drinking lemonade. And as I informed you at Lady Berriwell's, I was in complete control of my faculties." She turned to Lady Duggins with a smile. "You must excuse Mr. Worthington, my lady. He is a close friend of my family, so much so at times his behavior is that of a meddling, older brother."

Worth's mouth drew into a tight line.

"I've two brothers of my own, Lady Aurora." Lady Duggins sunk her fingers into Worth's arm. "I'm familiar."

"A pleasure seeing you, Lady Duggins. Mr. Worthington. If you'll excuse me, my chaperone, Miss Maplehurst, is waving for me to join her. Good evening."

Worth gave her a jerky bow, eyes gleaming like sapphires. Jaw so hard it could cut glass. He didn't care to be compared to one of her brothers. Well, he had it coming.

Approaching Aurora with Lady Duggins on his arm and then having the audacity to interject himself into the conversation with Mendenhall was beyond annoying. If he didn't want to agree to Aurora's proposal, so be it.

Worth may as well have slapped Aurora with one of his gloves and issued a formal challenge.

CHAPTER EIGHT

AURORA WALKED TEN paces down the path, turning only to cast a baleful glance at her chaperone. Aunt Lottie sat on a bench facing the pond some distance away, completely unperturbed to be sitting alone in Hyde Park while the dew still wet the grass.

"The need for subterfuge," Aurora murmured as she turned and took a few more steps, "is unnecessary."

Lord Kenebruke's carriage was scheduled to appear at any moment and would "accidentally" come upon Aunt Lottie. The entire tableau was somewhat silly given the age of the gentleman and lady in question. But Aunt Lottie said it created a bit of forbidden excitement, as if Kenebruke and Aunt Lottie were once more young lovers about to be caught by a disapproving matron.

Aurora continued down the path, plucking a leaf absently as she passed a shrub.

The trip to the park for an accidental meeting was all the more ridiculous given Lord Kenebruke called upon Aunt Lottie at Emerson House a few days after Lady Mormont's music recital.

Aurora stopped and batted at a pink bloom. The shrub was covered with them.

A grinning Lord Kenebruke had been ushered into the drawing room followed by his nephew and heir, Mr. Healey. Once they'd all taken a seat and Aurora sent Holly for tea, Lord Kenebruke stood and announced a walk around the garden was required to stretch out his leg.

Aunt Lottie, of course, accompanied him.

The next hour, Aurora was forced to entertain Healey, who thankfully, was an attractive, pleasant gentleman who shared her love of books. He commented on several tomes discarded on a side table, one of which was Jordan's book on animal husbandry. That led to less forced conversation until Kenebruke and Aunt Lottie returned.

There were no grass stains or leaves stuck to the older couple's clothing when they reappeared, but Aunt Lottie's cheeks were pink. When Kenebruke and his nephew took their leave, the elderly lord let it be known he took a carriage ride through Hyde Park every morning, before winking at Aunt Lottie.

Aurora pulled out the tiny watch she carried from her reticule and checked the time.

Each day promptly at nine o'clock. An hour when most, like Aurora, should still be lingering over hot chocolate.

Twice since Kenebruke's visit, Aunt Lottie decreed that she and Aurora would begin a new exercise regimen. One that involved walking down this exact path in Hyde Park, each day at exactly eight-thirty. The extra half hour gave Aunt Lottie plenty of time to perch on one of the benches, fluff her skirts and pretend absolute absorption in a novel. She never failed to gasp in surprise at seeing Kenebruke traveling through the park.

Aurora thought it some sort of game between the two.

A familiar carriage came around the bend, slowing as it neared the bench where Aunt Lottie sat. At least Kenebruke was prompt.

Aurora looked away and walked over to a spray of peonies that spilled along the edge of the path. Based on her past visits to the park, she should have brought her own book. Aunt Lottie often disappeared into Kenebruke's carriage. This might take some time.

"Have you lost Miss Maplehurst again?"

Her lips pursed slightly, though a tingle ran through her at the sound of Worth. Aurora did not immediately lift her nose from the peony. She was rather displeased with him given his behavior at the music recital. She hadn't spoken to him since, though Aurora had glimpsed Worth at a ball she'd attended with Jordan and Odessa a few nights ago, yet another lovely woman clinging to his arm.

Worth had lifted his head, catching sight of Aurora, considering her with an oddly thoughtful expression until she looked away. This entire week, after retiring for the night, she did nothing but stare at the pattern of the wallpaper in her room, wondering why she was so set on this course of action with Worth. Imploring a rake, a friend of her brother's no less, to indulge her curiosity. Tutor her.

I am somewhat ridiculous.

She should be grateful that Worth hadn't informed Jordan. Or perhaps Tamsin. But Aurora thought it telling that he had not.

"I don't lose Miss Maplehurst. Rather the other way around. She's just down the path, inside that carriage visiting a friend." Aurora retreated from the peony and turned.

Worth sat atop his horse, hair sparkling like gold in the sun, as if he were Apollo himself. The deep green of his coat was nearly the same color as the grass around them and his riding breeches stretched so tightly across the stretch of his muscular thighs Aurora had to momentarily look away. She wondered how Worth could sit a horse properly in such attire.

The sapphire gaze slid over Aurora but didn't linger on any of the obvious spots before regarding her with politeness, but little else.

How bloody disappointing.

"I stand corrected." Worth glanced in the direction of Kenebruke's carriage before returning to her. "Allow me to make introductions. This is Priscilla." He nodded to the horse, who snorted loudly in response.

"Priscilla?" Aurora moved closer, eyeing his mount. "Odd. Your horse isn't even a female."

"He's named for the headmaster's wife at Eton. Whom I despised. The headmaster, not his wife. I liked her quite a bit." A smirk crossed his mouth. "She liked to make me tarts, among other things. Let me mount you, Priscilla," he whispered to the horse. "I like riding you, Priscilla."

Aurora snorted before bursting into laughter. "You are terrible, Worth."

He had always been with her, at least before her debut. Almost as if Aurora's come out had somehow muted Worth's ability to jest with Aurora or partner her in cards. He no longer spoke of books with her. Or pretended to swoon when Jordan's wife, Odessa, launched into one of her morbid tales. She missed that Worth.

"There are noises coming from that carriage," Worth tilted his head. "Are you sure Miss Maplehurst is well?"

"Perfectly well." Aurora walked a bit further. Aunt Lottie deserved her privacy.

Worth gazed over her shoulder once more. "That is Lord Kenebruke's carriage."

"It is. Do you know him?"

"And his nephew." The corner of Worth's mouth tightened. "Mr. Healey. He inserts himself in his uncle's affairs."

"He is Kenebruke's heir. I would think that normal." Worth didn't like Mr. Healey, which was odd because Worth liked nearly everyone. "I find Mr. Healey lovely. He's come to Emerson House along with his uncle. He likes books nearly as much as I do." She paused as Worth's eyes rested on her face. "Mr. Healey has asked to call upon me."

He hadn't. Not exactly. But Mr. Healey had intimated that he would *ask* to call upon Aurora soon.

"Did he?" Something glinted in those sapphire depths before fading and he smiled once more. "He's rather staid for you, isn't he, Aurora?" Worth had managed to put Priscilla between the view of Kenebruke's carriage and the woods along the path, caging her in. The trees surrounding them created a thick canopy overhead. No one else was out due to the hour.

She and Worth were quite alone.

"I've brought you something to help—with your situation." The cool, sharply patrician tone softened. "I've debated over loaning this to you, but—I think it may satisfy some of your curiosity."

"But not you. You won't satisfy it."

Worth slid down from Priscilla and shook his head. "It isn't proper, Aurora. But I don't want you ruining yourself by asking questions or demonstrations of other gentlemen. They may not have your best interests at heart. I'll—do my best to answer some of your questions."

That was something, wasn't it?

Worth's eyes had darkened to indigo as he looked down at her, although it could have been merely an effect of the dappled sunlight coming through the trees. He appeared annoyed, but uncertain. Angry, but reluctant.

"We should talk about—" He looked away. "The maze. I apologize for not taking you seriously. But you smelled of rum punch."

Aurora clasped her hands behind her back and studied him, looking for any cracks in those perfectly shuttered features. Any indication of the same desire she'd glimpsed in the maze.

"You are here because of Lady Marmont's recital. You are concerned I would engage Mendenhall as a tutor, and not for the piano."

"I thought you might be foxed, as you were that day in the maze."

"I meant to kiss you, Worth," she stated plainly. "I wanted to for some time. And you kissed me back." Aurora's eyes drifted down the length of him.

"Don't do that."

Aurora raised a brow.

"You can't go about regarding a gentleman in such a manner."

"You aren't a gentleman."

He pierced her with a look, one that held a sharp flare of anger. "I most certainly am. Most of the time." Worth shrugged. "I was the day in the maze. A lesser man would have lifted your skirts. One who didn't care about you or your reputation."

Worth *cared* for her. Another something.

"You must know that I cannot agree to your request, Aurora. You are mad to think I would." Elegant fingers drummed along one thigh. "Simply because you think me safe and incapable of ruining you because I am your brother's friend." He paused. "*Your* friend."

"You are safe because you abhor the thought of marriage, and would take great care to be discreet and thus avoid that circumstance. You are vastly experienced. Satisfying my curiosity on you is far safer than say, Grisham, who I'm not sure I would wed if given the opportunity, though I find him appealing."

Worth shook his head.

"You need not fear a romantic entanglement with me, Worth."

A frown pulled at his lips. "Do not make such a proposal to anyone else. I mean it, Aurora."

Her natural inclination to disobedience almost had her informing Worth that he had no influence over her affairs, but Worth looked so stricken as he said the words. "I promise. Now, answer me one question. Why do you refuse to touch me?"

"I'm not refusing."

Aurora snorted. "You won't even take my hand in greeting. You didn't dance with me, not even at my come out." Her fingers trailed along the knuckles of one of his hands, feeling the elegant shape of his fingers beneath the leather gloves.

Worth inhaled sharply but did not pull away.

"Am I so unappealing?"

"Is that what you think? Foolish girl." Worth brought up his hand, jerking off one glove. "The truth is, I'm quite angry with you, Aurora."

The sight of that elegant hand, those long graceful fingers, sent a spill of longing down her spine. "Angry?"

"Furious."

Yes, she'd seen that. Something about her made Worth incredibly angry.

The nail of his thumb brushed lightly along the edge of her modest neckline, ruffling the bits of lace. He hadn't touched her skin, just the lace and piping, but even so, Aurora shivered with pleasure in that patch of sunlight. When his thumb delved gently into the valley between her breasts, Aurora's knees buckled. She arched in his direction, willing his fingers to slide over her entire body.

Worth leaned over, his breath teasing at the fine hairs around her ear. "I should give you your gift."

A pulse of heat flowed down the length of her neck from Worth's touch. Aurora had so hoped he'd relent, and her gift would be contact. Kissing. Stroking. Quite possibly, this is why he hesitated to touch her. There was such—eroticism to the mere glance of a finger when paired with desire one already felt. An effortless seduction. It didn't help that Worth smelled utterly delicious. She wanted to bury her nose in his coat.

The fingers retracted, and Worth reached into the pocket of his coat. "Hopefully, this will satisfy your inquisitive nature." Worth pulled out a square wrapped in plain paper, looking smug. "A book."

"A book. You've brought me a book." After making her knees weaken with just the barest touch, Worth had brought her a bloody book.

"Don't open the package until you are home and in the privacy of your room. The tome is rather scandalous, but highly educational. It should answer all your questions. Far better than I can. This book isn't one you can walk into Tate's and request. You might find it rather shocking in nature."

"I doubt it." She took the slim tome from his hand, noting that he was careful not to so much as brush a finger along hers.

"Aunt Lottie has a rather extensive collection."

Worth shut his eyes as if praying for divine assistance. "I understand your curiosity, but cannot indulge it. Except with this." He nodded to the book, eyes sparkling and somber. "I hope you can understand."

What Aurora understood was that Worth's coat barely hid the fact that he was aroused, but refused to act on it. "I suppose Grisham or Healey might permit a liberty or two." She plucked the book from his fingers.

"Aurora." His voice lowered. "This is a dangerous game you seek to play with me. Neither of us will win. And—it must cease. For your sake. What happened in the maze cannot ever happen again. Do you understand?"

What Aurora *did* understand was that Worth was pushing her away once more, though he clearly—she snuck a look at the edge of his coat once more—desired her. But he wasn't going to act on that desire.

"Very well. Thank you for the gift."

"You are welcome, Aurora." He turned back to her and tugged the edge of his coat down, features composed. Polite. "I hope this puts an end to your—curiosity."

Aurora's gaze flicked down Worth's long legs, slowly moving back to his chest. The riding breeches he wore were *terribly* unforgiving. He might be reluctant, but parts of him were not. "I'll be sure to let you know," she said as he once more mounted Priscilla, "if I have any questions."

"Please do not," Worth said stiffly. "I bid you good morning, Lady Aurora."

She clasped the book to her chest. "Good morning, Mr. Worthington."

RESTRAINT.

That was the word Charles decided on as he rode away from

Aurora. He was rather proud he had any at all left when it came to her. Drawing a thumb along the edge of her delicious bosom had Charles coming undone, but he'd had the strength to pull back.

Taking a deep breath, he welcomed the smell of horse and leather as he headed to the other side of the park, begging it to wipe away the scent of honeysuckle on Aurora's skin. The feel of her skin, like the finest silk, had nearly driven him mad. Charles had wanted to press his mouth between those firm mounds. Ease his tongue between those lovely globes of flesh.

He rode past another spray of peonies shining a dusky rose in the morning sun.

Were Aurora's nipples the same shade?

He urged Priscilla into a gallop, putting as much distance as he could between his cock and Aurora Sinclair. Charles could have taken her right there, in the wet grass. And she would have allowed it.

This is why he could not touch Aurora. Ever again.

CHAPTER NINE

A URORA SIPPED HER tea, added more sugar, and casually took in the Duchess of Ware. Her Grace struggled to sit upright on the settee, with little success. All that flopping about had only managed to tangle her in the silk of her skirts. Rather like an enormous turtle who cannot manage to get back on its feet. Her sister would not appreciate the comparison.

"Tamsin, should you be out paying calls given," she gestured pointedly to Tamsin's overly large stomach, "your condition?"

"I'm perfectly fine." A frustrated sound came from her as she finally managed to right herself, pushing a pillow beneath each arm with a grunt to hold herself in place. "I needed a moment of respite. Ware is smothering me. Like one of his bloody moths. When he isn't about, the dowager's ancient butler follows me, hands out, bracing himself in case I fall." Tamsin's eyes drew up to her brows. "As if he could catch me. He's at least eighty with bones more brittle than the china."

Aurora bit her lip, trying not to laugh. Poor Tamsin. Ware was rather terrifying when intent on the protection of his wife and child. "His fear is warranted given the number of cats inhabiting your home. You might trip." The Dowager Duchess of Ware was well known for her love of felines. There must be at least a dozen inhabiting the duke's mansion.

"I had to sneak out." Tamsin thumped a pillow with her fist. "Forced to bribe one of the footmen so as not to alert the household I was leaving." She wiggled about, trying to get comfortable which was nearly impossible given her condition. "This is Ware's fault. All of it. Make me a plate, Aurora. Escaping a duke makes one quite hungry."

Aurora took a small plate and filled it with two scones and a biscuit, handing it to her sister who promptly placed the bounty atop the mound of her stomach.

"These smell quite delicious." Tamsin inhaled. "I'm starving."

"Well, I rather think you might have had something to do with it. You can't blame Ware completely." Alyss, Malcolm's wife, perched in a chair, her ever-present parasol leaning to the side, dark eyes observing the mountain that was Tamsin.

"At least I wasn't ruined in a cottage while pretending to be someone else." Tamsin bit into a scone viciously. "Waving about a parasol. As if that would frighten anyone, let alone, Malcom."

Alyss raised a pale brow, not the least put off by Tamsin's comments. "The ruination occurred *after* I revealed my identity," she corrected. "Not before. Malcolm knew perfectly well who I was. And as for parasol injuries, I can give you a list of my cousin's former suitors." She smiled sweetly.

"You're merely grumpy, Tamsin," Odessa, chimed in. "Because you haven't had anything stronger than tea in ages. Not even a glass of ratafia."

"The smell of spirits," Tamsin declared, "makes my stomach pitch. Trust me, I long for just a sip of good, Irish whiskey. Dream of it. Ware poured a glass and—well the results were not promising. I think I may have ruined his boots and scared the half-dozen cats surrounding me. Also, I would like to point out, I am not paying a call. Only visiting my family. Besides, if something happens," she waved a hand in a circular motion around the giant mound of her stomach, "Holly will carry me up the stairs and send for the physician, won't you, Holly?"

Holly, the Emerson butler, inclined his large head. Rather like a mastiff who ushered in guests. "Yes, Your Grace." He adored Tamsin and would likely have the child for her if he could.

"I read the most provocative story, just the other day." Odessa, eyes gleaming, took a bite of a biscuit. "There is a werewolf in Northumberland. Spotted very near Spittal. Carried off two sheep." She paused, eyes wide, waiting for their reaction to the news. "Close to *Dunnings.*"

"We are all aware," Tamsin chewed her scone, "where Dunnings is located, Odessa."

Aurora had also read a provocative story the other day, though it had little to do with strange beasts roaming Northumberland eating sheep, and a great deal to do with naked limbs and the correct position for one's mouth to perform a particular sexual act. The book Worth had loaned her was more memoir than anything else. Quite titillating.

She took a shaky sip of her tea as a light pulse drifted between her thighs.

"Dunnings is nothing but coal now. No sheep," Aurora said to Odessa, determined to keep her mind free of such arousing thoughts while sipping tea with her sister. "And there is no such thing as a werewolf."

Aurora adored Odessa, but her fascination with the macabre and other grotesque tales, mostly concerning criminals and their executions, took getting accustomed to. There had been a period of time when each household member including poor Holly and Mrs. Cherry, the cook, had to sit for a wax masque. A project of Odessa's based on her love of the wax creations of Madame Tussaud. Mrs. Cherry had nearly quit after finding a wax head of one of the footmen in the larder. But since the birth of little Douglas, her tastes had veered to the more fantastical. Hell hounds. Ghosts. Winged things.

"There is. I read an eyewitness report. Apparently, the werewolf took up two sheep in its jaws," Odessa opened her mouth wide, "snapped their necks and—"

"Good grief, Odessa." Alyss laughed. "There isn't a monster in Northumberland running about and eating sheep."

"Says you who live in a house haunted by ghosts." Odessa sat back with a small huff.

"*Reputed* to be haunted." Alyss calmly sipped her tea. Very few things ruffled Alyss. Malcolm mostly, but little else.

"What about those things in the desert you are always going on about?"

"Djinn," Alyss replied in a solemn tone. "I don't joke about them. When I lived in the desert as a child, djinn were known to take the shape of a sandstorm. The sand would invade our tent, nearly drowning us. The djinn wanted our souls."

"My mother believed in fairies," Tamsin said before devouring the rest of her scones. "Aurora, hold a cup of tea to my lips. I can't reach it." The plate on her stomach listed to the side.

She dutifully picked up the teacup and placed it against Tamsin's mouth so her sister could take a sip.

"So why not a werewolf?" Odessa countered. "If you believe in djinn or ghosts?"

"I never said I believed in ghosts, only that our home was reputed to have them."

This is what tea had become at Emerson House. A strange discussion of imaginary beasts instead of ordinary gossip.

"A spirit that takes the shape of wind? You'll agree to that but not a bloody werewolf?" Tamsin seemed determined to annoy Alyss today.

Alyss stroked her parasol.

"Don't try to badger me with that thing. The djinns can stay in the desert. Nor do I care about overly large wolves. I'm married to one." Tamsin fell back against the settee, plate now only full of crumbs. "I'm rather out of sorts today. And I'm exhausted. This," she thumped her stomach and Aurora reached over quickly to snatch the teetering plate, "is all rather tiring. I only wanted to visit to see how and if things were progressing with Aurora's gentlemen callers. There's two at last count. Which is two more than I ever had."

Aurora glared at Holly, who had the decency to look ashamed. He was supposed to keep such things to himself. She should have known he would tell Tamsin whatever she wished to know. He always did. But she'd expected better of Odessa.

And now Alyss knew, which meant both Grisham and Healey would be thoroughly investigated.

Traitors.

Odessa merely shrugged.

She supposed this was far better, to have the family's attention on Healey or Grisham rather than Worth. Whom she had not seen since he'd given her the explicit, shockingly detailed memoir of an infamous courtesan. He had been notably absent from the variety of parties and balls she'd attended. Purposefully, Aurora surmised. If Worth assumed *The Bloom of the Rose* would shock her into modesty, his plan had failed miserably. Aurora was now more curious than ever. The tome had only given her already fertile imagination that much more to consider.

"Aurora?" Tamsin pinched her. "Goodness, the look on your face. Someone has made an impression. Tell me all about it."

Yes, someone had made quite the impression on Aurora: Miss Rose Wildenhurst. Author of *The Bloom of the Rose*. A young girl of sixteen who decides her true calling is to become London's finest courtesan. Even Aunt Lottie would blush reading Rose's recounting. Which begged the question of why Worth had given it to her.

Another flutter between her thighs took up residence. Aurora imagined Worth in every scenario recounted in *The Bloom of the Rose*.

"I've been paid a total of three calls," she said carefully. "One by Lord Grisham and two by Mr. Healey. He is the nephew and heir of Lord Kenebruke."

"Lord Kenebruke?" Alyss asked in a suspicious tone. "I'm not familiar."

An investigation was about to begin. Alyss tended to be *overprotective*, particularly when it came to a young lady and her suitors. Her skills at gathering information were incredibly useful, considering Malcolm investigated for various members of society.

Mostly corrupt relatives or spousal affairs, unless he was doing work for Lord Curchon which he never discussed with anyone.

"Mr. Healey does not need further inquiry, Alyss. Nor your parasol." Alyss had a reputation for swatting the overly amorous gentlemen. "He's perfectly well-mannered. Staid, if you will. Lord Kenebruke is an earl from Northumberland, as it happens. Mr. Healey accompanied his uncle when Kenebruke called on Aunt Lottie. He likes books."

"All true. I was here when Lord Kenebruke arrived, but I had an appointment with the modiste and did not stay." Odessa's gaze held a question for Aurora. "Lovely gentleman, though I am unaware of my aunt's history with Kenebruke. Did they become acquainted recently?"

Aurora gave her an innocent look. "I'm not certain." Kenebruke was Aunt Lottie's story to tell, not hers. If she hadn't confided in Odessa, there was likely a reason.

"And Lord Grisham?" Tamsin's eyes glinted. "Ware claims he's a bit chilly. Something of a prig."

"Ware is a bit chilly," Aurora reminded her. "And Lord Grisham is not a prig. Merely reserved." Slightly boring. Lacked a sense of humor. But she didn't add that part.

"Polite and intelligent, if a bit quiet," Odessa added. "Well behaved."

"Well behaved? He isn't a dog, is he?" Alyss bit into a biscuit. "I know all about Grisham."

Thank goodness.

"Healey," Odessa ignored Alyss's comment, "in my opinion, is more the prig. I thought him rigid."

"You decided to relate the gruesome details of a pirate's execution and he objected," Aurora shot back in annoyance. "It is hardly something one discusses at a first meeting, Odessa, let alone over tea. His discomfort at the topic does not make him a prig."

Aurora *liked* Healey, though he wasn't Worth. But still Aurora thought she should defend him. If Healey was just a trifle less polite, she would like him even more. "At any rate, I'm not sure if either will suit me well enough to wed."

At Grisham's hand taking hers in greeting at the Wymouth ball, Aurora had felt an excessively mild, tingle in her arm, but nothing else. Healey created a bit more warmth in her mid-section, but further time in his company or a kiss would be more helpful to determine his suitability. Aurora hated to admit to it but both gentlemen were somewhat prudish, but perhaps that was merely for her benefit. That was why a liberty or two would be required. Grisham especially seemed to have a stick shoved up his rather perfect—

Aurora clasped her hands and took a deep breath.

A proper young lady wouldn't be focused on a man's masculine form. Or compare Grisham and Healey to the magnificent, goldenly graceful, Charles Worthington.

You couldn't simply gift a young lady an overly detailed memoir from a courtesan and assume the matter settled.

Goodness, London was littered with rakes. Any one of them would have agreed to Aurora's proposal without a second thought. She should have found one of them.

"Whatever are you thinking about?" Tamsin murmured, eyes slowly narrowing into slits. She'd be snoring in moments.

Holly really needed to summon Ware and have her taken home.

"I was considering the contrary nature of human beings. Saying one thing but meaning and doing the complete opposite." Like insisting you didn't want to kiss or touch someone when you so obviously *did*.

A tiny snort came from her sister's parted lips.

Tamsin was obviously no longer listening. Not that she would be any help at all, only horrified that Aurora had made such a proposal to Worth. Her sister had never really liked him, no matter that he was Drew's business partner. If she found out Worth had given Aurora a courtesan's memoir, or Aurora asked to be tutored in pleasure—

"She's fallen asleep again," Odessa said softly. Standing, she eyed Tamsin's stomach. "Do you think there's more than one tucked inside? Twins run in the Sinclair family. I was rather disappointed I had only the one child but—"

"You are *obsessed*, Odessa." Alyss rolled her eyes. "I promise you that if Malcolm is receiving," she waved a hand around her temple, "messages from Andrew with his mind or they spoke in a special language, I would tell you instantly. There is nothing *overtly* interesting about twins."

"It is only that she is—as large as a ship in Her Majesty's navy. And I disagree on your opinion of twins. They are endlessly fascinating."

"Spend the day with Malcolm while he cleans his pistols, and you may feel differently."

Odessa pursed her lips. "I'll send you one of my pamphlets that details—"

"Please do not." Alyss set down her cup. "I beg you."

"Holly," Odessa kept her voice low. "Send for the duke to collect his duchess."

The remainder of the conversation centered around Odessa's efforts to hold a ghost hunting expedition at the home of Alyss and Malcolm, if only so she could ascertain whether their house was indeed haunted.

Alyss always refused.

Finally, giving up, Odessa turned to Aurora.

"Where has my aunt gotten off to this afternoon? I had thought she'd join us for tea. Out walking again? She never liked the park so much until recently."

Aurora gave a careless shrug. "I'm not sure. She told me her dresses were becoming too tight and instituted an exercise regimen. Too many scones."

"Hmm." Odessa had the most arresting eyes. Shrewd and the color of wet slate. Piercing. As if she were plotting your demise or busy staring into your soul. Jordan, and nearly everyone else, found it difficult to keep anything a secret with Odessa. Aurora was amazed Aunt Lottie had.

"My aunt has never expressed a desire to curb her like of scones. Does this have to do with Kenebruke?"

"I—"

A curse sounded from the entrance of the drawing room and Aurora was thankfully spared from further interrogation by the arrival of the Duke of Ware. He made not a sound as he entered the room to take in his sleeping wife, which was impressive, given his size.

Another snore came from Tamsin.

"Stubborn thing," Ware said, adoration stamped on his features. "She needs to stay home until the child comes."

"Or children," Odessa interjected.

Ware gave her an exasperated look. Odessa and the duke were cousins in a roundabout way and shared a love of oddities. Fascination with twins being one. "Stop being so hopeful, Odessa. The physician claims there is only one."

"He could be wrong."

"Your Grace." Alyss stood. "I'll follow you out. Malcolm will be wondering where I've gotten off to. And Emilia will be up from her nap."

"Kiss my niece for me," Aurora said. Emelia was an adorable little thing. She had Alyss's nearly white, blonde hair and Malcolm's green eyes. She resembled a tiny, woodland elf.

Odessa came to her feet as well. "I need to go over the dinner menu with Mrs. Cherry and check on Douglas. He's probably waiting for a story." Odessa read penny dreadfuls to Douglas, claiming there was no harm since he couldn't possibly understand what she was saying at his age.

"Do you want to come with me?" Odessa stared at her, as if able to discern Aunt Lottie's secrets from reading Aurora's thoughts.

"I believe I'll take a nap," she answered with a yawn. "I didn't sleep well last night."

Aurora had barely been sleeping at all. It was impossible after reading portions of *The Bloom of the Rose* to have a restful sleep. Not when your mind was full of questions and your body aroused. Every nerve in her body felt tight, like the strings of a violin just waiting to be plucked.

Good grief.

A tremor ran through her as the drawing room emptied and Aurora was left alone. A plan had been forming as she listened to Tamsin snore while Odessa and Alyss debated the existence of ghosts, one that was daring, reckless, and highly improper.

Aurora had questions, of a sensitive nature. And hadn't Worth said he would answer those questions when giving her the book?

CHAPTER TEN

"**S**IR, YOU HAVE a caller."

Charles looked up from the ledgers and correspondence divided into neat stacks on his desk. He had just been about to write a rebuttal to that pest Healey, who seemed determined to stick his nose into the deal Charles was working on with Lord Kenebruke. The older earl had asked him to allow Healey his inquiries, after all, his nephew would inherit one day and needed preparation.

Charles was trying. Honestly. But Healey was something of a nitwit.

"Whoever it is, send them away. I'm busy at present and not at home."

He had neglected to tell Aurora the complete truth when claiming only a slight acquaintance with Lord Kenebruke.

Kenebruke owned a textile mill, one he'd received as part of his wife's dowry ages ago. The mill needed a great deal of work to make it profitable once more. The equipment was outdated and Kenebruke had no desire to spend the sum needed to modernize the mill.

Drew had first spotted the opportunity after meeting with a gentleman in London, Mr. Swift, who was focused on producing ready-made clothing to be sold to the burgeoning middle class. The demand for such clothing would soon outpace the supply, especially as more people left the countryside to take employment in the larger cities. After some consideration, a visit to the mill, and thorough inspection of the legers, Kenebruke and his textile mill was designated as a good investment. Kenebruke would remain a partner, though his share would be greatly reduced. Drew and Charles would fund the modernization as well as handle the agreements with Mr. Swift.

Until Kenebruke's pompous, idiotic nephew, Mr. Healey inserted himself.

"Sir." His butler, Ropely, returned once more.

Charles ignored him.

Despite knowing nothing about textiles, dyes, the market for ready-made clothing, or cotton importing, Healey had cast himself in the role of his uncle's protector, because of Kenebruke's age. He inferred that Kenebruke's mind was not as sharp as it had been in his youth and thus any business matters required his oversight.

Patently untrue.

Kenebruke's mind was sharp. His assessments sound. Healey only wished to put his stamp on everything in a bid to exert his control over the situation. Kenebruke allowed it out of affection for his nephew.

"The young lady is quite insistent." Ropely didn't move from where he stood at the door. "Lady Aurora Sinclair," he said in a low tone.

Charles pushed back from his desk, his annoyance at Healey momentarily forgotten. What on earth was Aurora doing here? Alone and unescorted? He'd taken great pains to avoid her since lending her that tome, hoping that would put an end to the situation. Granted, it hadn't for Charles. Aurora still haunted him. Far too often.

"I've taken the precaution of calling the staff to the kitchens. The condition of the guest rooms must be discussed." Ropely inclined his head.

There wasn't anything wrong with the guestrooms as they were rarely used. Bless Ropely.

"I took the initiative of putting Lady Aurora in the drawing room, Mr. Worthington."

"Very good, Ropely. I'll be along directly." Charles stood. He'd taken off his coat and rolled up his sleeves while he worked and reached to retrieve the garment, but then decided not to bother. Lady Aurora Sinclair was not going to be here long enough for it to matter.

If she had questions of a personal nature, then Miss Maplehurst could damn well answer them.

Charles had assured himself *The Bloom of the Rose* was an inspired choice for a young lady of Aurora's overly curious nature. Shock some sense into her. The tome was rather descriptive and detailed. Any young lady in her second Season would faint dead away at the recounting of the various acts a courtesan was required to perform. At the time, Charles had seen it as his only recourse. He couldn't allow Aurora to throw herself at the likes of Grisham nor could he have Aurora practicing her wiles on him. Or teach her the myriad of wicked things—

He ran a hand through his hair.

Charles had some vague hope that *The Bloom of the Rose* would satisfy Aurora's curiosity enough so that she would put it aside until she was properly wed. Her questions and experimentation would involve her future husband. Aurora should be so taken aback by the explicit carnality in *The Bloom of the Rose* that she would be far too embarrassed to ever broach the subject with Charles again. Their relationship could once more return to distant politeness.

It is possible, given her appearance today, Charles had underestimated Aurora.

"Would serve me right if Malcolm pointed a pistol at my head or Emerson beat me to a pulp," he said under his breath. "Drew will kick me in the ribs."

Or more likely, Emerson would require Charles and Aurora wed.

He forced the very thought out of his head.

Not the least put out by his musings, his cock was overjoyed to know Aurora was waiting, stiffening to marble at the mere thought of her in his drawing room. He should have worn his coat after all. A hum was lighting across his skin, stirring at his arousal in a vicious manner.

I'm a rake. I'm too old for her. I don't want to marry. Her brothers will murder me.

Charles silently chanted the words while Ropely led the way to the drawing room, instructing his cock to stand down, or at the very least, not be so noticeable.

"Lady Aurora." He stepped into the drawing room, the delicate sweet scent of honeysuckle immediately filing his nostrils. Aurora's petite, rounded form—

Christ, those curves.

—sat perched on the edge of the settee. Hands tightly clasped in her lap. Her chin tilted toward Charles as he entered, the bits of green in her hazel eyes sharpening at the sight of him.

"Good afternoon, Mr. Worthington." Aurora looked quite fierce sitting on those tufted silk cushions, tapping one foot impatiently. Determination, an abundance of it, lit her beautiful features.

Charles wavered. The same determination with which he'd seen in the maze. His cock pulsed in his trousers, completely pleased to see Aurora.

Not now.

He'd been at the mercy of his cock for more than half his life. He supposed most men were. Terrible weakness.

Ropely closed the drawing room door with a soft click.

"You shouldn't be here, unescorted in the middle," Charles took a deep breath trying not to inhale the sweet honeysuckle clinging to her, "of the bloody afternoon. I'll have my carriage brought around to take you home."

"There's no need to curse, Worth. And I'm not returning home, not until I've had an opportunity to to speak to you about this." Reaching beside her, Aurora pulled out *The Bloom of the*

Rose.

"Shocking, isn't it?"

"Incredibly," Aurora agreed.

"You wish to return the book to me and never speak of this again. I quite understand." He moved forward, not bothering to examine why some tiny part of him was…disappointed?

"Shocking is a tame description. This book," she lifted the slim tome, "is quite *filthy* in nature, Worth. There are illustrations along with details that would make even Aunt Lottie blush. And she has an entire collection of rather scandalous works. But none reaching these heights. Hers are rather mild in comparison."

Charles wasn't the least shocked to know that Miss Maplehurst, the worst sort of chaperone for a young lady such as Aurora, had her own collection of erotic works. "I'm sorry, Aurora, for offending you with such reading material. I'm sure you can see now why it would be best to take any remaining questions to Miss Maplehurst, or better, wait until you are wed and can explore"—he stumbled over the word—"these things with a husband. I'll take it back and we can forget—"

"On the contrary," Aurora drawled, interrupting his speech. "Further discussion is merited."

"Further discussion?" Charles didn't care for the mischievous smile pulling at her lips. Nor the fact that her breasts, those delightful mounds he *salivated over*, kept threatening to burst out of her bodice with each breath she took.

"Chapter four." Aurora smacked the slim, leather clad tome on the table before her.

Charles wracked his brain. He had no idea what was in chapter four, though if it was that close to beginning of *The Bloom of the Rose*, the situation couldn't be too depraved. The debauchery worsened the further one read as Rose experienced a variety of sexual pleasures.

He plucked the book from Aurora's fingers and riffled through the pages until he reached the beginning of the chapter.

Bloody hell.

Charles looked away, his resolve shredded. Desire for Aurora ached along his skin. His fingers curled into fists at his side to keep from touching her.

That bloody book was the worst idea I've ever had.

"You need to leave. Immediately." A surge of absolute lust heated beneath his skin at the thought of tasting—

"I disagree." Aurora lifted her skirts, exposing a pair of slender calves encased in silk. "Chapter four."

CHAPTER ELEVEN

A URORA'S BRAVADO WOULD not falter. She refused to allow Worth to push her out the door, not without some sort of satisfactory conclusion.

Chapter four was as far as she'd read thus far, deliberately choosing not to read any further. Instead, Aurora had reread this portion of *The Bloom of the Rose* repeatedly for the past few days, and again only moments ago on the carriage ride to Worth's. There was a reason she hadn't been sleeping well at night.

Worth on his knees before her.

That golden head wedged between her thighs.

She nearly tore her skirts in her haste to lift them.

A sound fell from his lips. Slightly feral and not at all like the elegant, charming rake Aurora had come to know. The blue of his eyes darkened so dramatically Aurora could no longer make out the pupils. He stared pointedly at the spot between her thighs.

"Lift your skirts higher," he rasped softly. "Or *leave*."

Arousal sifted low in Aurora's mid-section, her body responding to that command given in such a low, dangerous timbre. She obeyed without hesitation, only pausing when he spoke once more.

"Stop. Do so slowly."

"I don't think—" Aurora meant to ask what moving the fabric up her legs at a snail's pace had to do with anything. She was far more curious about what came after her skirts were up around her waist.

"Chapter four, Aurora. *Specifically*, page twenty-six." Worth's voice held just a touch of menace.

Bits of sensation lit across her skin at the sound of him. "Page twenty-six," she repeated stupidly.

"Do you wish it or not?" Worth drew in a long breath, the look in his eyes mildly frightening. As if he'd tear her apart with his teeth.

Good lord, she would let him. Desire washed over her in a wave. She nodded. "Yes."

"Then do as I ask."

Slowly, Aurora pulled the fabric of her skirts upward, every brush of the silk tickling her calves in a sensual caress. The lace at the hem of her skirts caught against her stockings, dragging in a seductive manner until she paused the hem at her knees. Her nipples tightened into small, painful buds. The pulse in her neck fluttered so dramatically, Aurora was sure Worth could see it.

Worth waved his hand. "Up."

Aurora rucked her skirts higher, stopping again at her waist.

"Keep it there. Don't let go. Part your thighs."

Aurora inhaled softly, hesitating only a moment before she obeyed. She had never felt so exposed in her life.

His eyed drifted down the length of her form to her splayed legs, fixing on the soft tuft of hair over her mound. Worth came down to his knees before the settee, wedging his larger body between her legs. His lashes fluttered over the sharp line of his cheeks. A deep sigh, one of restrained longing came from him. Worth's beautiful, graceful hands trailed over the silk-clad length of her legs, pausing to trace the delicate curve of her ankles, before gently exploring the lines of her knees.

"Worth."

"Don't make a sound."

One palm stretched over her thigh, warm and solid, holding her in place. Leaning forward, he blew a light stream of air over the soft hair covering her sex.

Aurora gasped softly, jolting at the unfamiliar, sinful feel of his breath.

"Page twenty-six," he whispered. "It has been some time since I've read *The Bloom of the Rose*. I'd forgotten her encounter with a nameless gentleman before she leaves home. He seduces her in the drawing room." The fingers of his free hand tangled in the hair covering her mound, tugging gently. "With his mouth."

"Yes, and I—Lady Bryant seemed so enamored of this act, that day in the maze and—"

"She is unimportant." Worth's chin dipped without warning, his tongue moving along her exposed flesh, lazily traveling through her folds. Licking gently. Savoring her. A most marvelous sensation that traveled up and down her limbs.

Aurora fell back against the cushions of the settee.

Worth groaned, pressing his lips more fully against her. The pad of his tongue moved, teasing along the small bit of flesh now open to him. With great care, Worth parted her folds, his breath warm and gentle, like the kiss of a butterfly.

Aurora's body sharpened. The ache between her thighs that much more pronounced and insistent. She melted for Worth, her legs splaying further of their own accord.

"Don't take your eyes from me, Aurora," he murmured, the words vibrating seductively along her folds. "I want to ensure I answer all of your questions." One big hand stretched possessively over her stomach, holding her in place. "I don't want to leave anything out."

"Don't you dare," Aurora whimpered. The sight of his blonde head nestled deep inside the curls between her thighs had her toes curling within her slippers.

Worth caught her eyes, drawing his tongue over the engorged flesh at Aurora's center. Circling the tiny nub until Aurora clutched at the settee cushions. "Tell me what feels best." He licked and sucked, pausing only to watch her again. "So you can find your pleasure."

"All of it, Worth," she panted, frustrated he'd stopped. "I like all of it."

"Have you ever climaxed before, Aurora?" Teeth grazed at her flesh, and she jerked, before he lightly sucked and teased once more. "Don't lie."

"Yes. But—at least I think so." She'd fumbled about in the bath, toying with soap and sponge. Used her fingers. But the relief she experienced, the pleasure she wanted, was never equal to its promise. "I didn't know what I was doing. I wanted more."

His tongue flicked, eliciting another whimper from her. "Well, this should give you something to aspire to."

Chapter ten was Devoted to a Woman's Release in *the Bloom of the Rose*, But Aurora Only Paged Through It, Considering That She Knew Something of the Topic Already. Also, She was Determined Not to Read So Far Ahead. Rose Had Insisted That This Particular Act, One Practiced on Her by That Nameless Gentleman, was What Made Her Decide on a Life As a Courtesan. The Pleasure was Beyond Describing, If a Man Didn't Flounder About and Knew What He was Doing.

Like Worth.

Aurora writhed, her hips shifting about. The bliss inside her crashed and roared almost to completion before retreating once more. She wanted—

"Not yet." His tongue traveled further away from the spot craving his attention. "I'm not sure what you think you're doing, visiting me in the middle of the day."

"You said you would answer some of my questions. I had a bloody question." Aurora's breathing had grown ragged. She was shocked to find her fingers tangled in Worth's hair.

"I did." He sucked gently. "But I won't have your reputation shredded. You can't just come here unescorted without at least sending a note. Do you want to alert half of London to your descent into wickedness?"

"I don't care," she choked feeling as if her entire body, her impending pleasure, was being held in place by Worth.

"Yes, but I do." He chuckled as he eased one finger inside her. "Don't be so careless again."

Oh, she'd forgotten. This was part of page twenty-six or rather, twenty-seven. Fingers thrusting inside a woman's channel. There was a spot, tiny and well hidden inside her. The man's mouth—"Worth."

He curled his finger, rubbing gently back and forth at that deep spot until Aurora sobbed. Pulled at his hair, his shoulders, anything to urge him on. Her hips pushed more firmly against his mouth. Worth pulled one of Aurora's legs over his shoulder, spreading her further, and she let out a cry. Her pleasure was pushed and pulled; left to falter before being stoked into a searing flame once more. Aurora pleaded. Begged. "Please Worth."

"Come for me, beautiful creature," he murmured against her thigh, before his finger pressed and curled inside her while his mouth—*dear god his mouth*—sucked that small nub between his lips until she felt the graze of his teeth.

Her back arched sharply, threatening to snap suddenly, just as that crimson ribbon had in the maze. The rush of sensation, of pleasure was so swift and blinding, Aurora's breath halted in her lungs. Animalistic sounds came from her and she turned her head, screaming into the plush settee, praying Worth's servants didn't hear her.

Oh. I don't think I have properly pleasured myself. Or at all.

"Breathe, Aurora."

Another wave crashed over her, and his name tumbled from her lips in one long, glorious moan, as her limbs jerked. His mouth and tongue pressed her forward, until the tremors subsided, leaving Aurora with nothing but a magnificent feeling of satiety.

Stirring, Aurora reached for his hand.

Worth's fingers slipped from hers. The warmth of his mouth and body faded away. He came to his feet slowly, without looking at her, and walked to the other side of the room to stand beside one of the chairs.

Distance. Worth wants distance from me.

A hard, flinty gaze was thrown in her direction. His breathing was rough. His trousers were tented, giving an idea of the size of Worth's—and he was bloody furious.

"Worth." Aurora struggled to sit up. She felt a bit woozy, all things considered. And all she wanted after the most intense pleasure she'd ever experienced was him.

"If my explanation of chapter four and page twenty-six has been to your satisfaction, Lady Aurora, I have business to return to. Leave the damned book. I should never have given it to you."

"Then why did you?" Aurora stood, ignoring the way her legs wobbled like a bowl of aspic. "No, don't answer. I know why you gave it to me. You want me, Worth, as much as I—"

"Not another bloody word, Aurora," he snarled.

"This is coming with me." She picked up the book still sitting on the table. "I'm not finished with my research."

"Aurora."

Goodness, Worth sounded quite savage, unsurprising, she decided, given the tight stretch of his trousers. Aurora on the other hand, felt wonderful. Still in a euphoric daze, she managed to make it to the drawing room door. She waited for shame or mortification to engulf her, but those feelings were absent. There wasn't even any guilt at challenging Worth and pushing him over the edge.

Aurora placed her hand on the door, daring to turn and take one last look at Worth. He hadn't moved. He was right about one thing. This was a dangerous game between them. She wasn't sure how it should end.

Maybe it never would.

"Good day, Mr. Worthington. I'll see myself out."

CHAPTER TWELVE

TWO DAYS LATER, at exactly three o'clock in the afternoon, Charles poured himself a much-needed brandy after the negotiations he'd just gone through for a piece of property in Manchester and turned to see that Aurora once more invaded his drawing room.

Once more, she sat calmly on the settee, not even put off when he stated plainly for her to leave.

Charles was going to have a pointed discussion with Ropely. More importantly, how was Aurora evading her chaperone and visiting Charles?

"Chapter three. Page seventeen."

He had no idea what page seventeen contained, just as he hadn't page twenty-six. If she'd left the book behind, as he asked her, Charles would have studied the blasted thing.

Dressed in green sprigged muslin, Aurora resembled nothing so much as a lovely spring day. So lovely an ache filled his chest at the sight of her. One tiny curl dangled above her ear tempting him to press his lips to the spot and tug on that chestnut curl.

Dear God, everything about Aurora tempted him.

"You," he snarled, "should not be here."

Not put off by his tone and unwelcoming manner, Aurora merely brandished *The Bloom of the Rose*, holding it up like some bloody shield. "I have questions."

"Get your answers elsewhere."

"Very well. I suppose I could read passages of this book to Grisham. He's staid, but I'm sure with the correct incentive, he might be convinced. I'd probably end up wed to him. I suppose being a countess won't be so terrible." She made to stand.

Charles growled. He couldn't stop it. "What is on page seventeen?" he hissed, knowing she'd defeated him once more.

"I'm to sit in your lap. But if you are so opposed, I can sit on Healey's lap." She shrugged as if it didn't matter.

He held out his hand for the book.

Aurora gave him an innocent smile and opened the book to the pages she'd bookmarked.

The next hour was spent in pleasant torture with Aurora on his lap, grinding her backside against his cock. Charles thrust his fingers deep inside her while his thumb toyed with the small button hidden in her folds. He nipped at her neck, tugging at the honeysuckle scented skin with his teeth.

Aurora screamed out her release, bucking wildly against his thighs.

Thankfully, Ropely although delinquent in his duty to refuse Aurora entry, had the decency to call yet another staff meeting in the kitchens.

Before he could stop her, Aurora once more left with *The Bloom of the Rose* tucked into her reticule. The deliberate twitch of her hips as she sailed out of his drawing room left Charles with little doubt that she would be back. He was left unbelievably hard and aroused, shocked at his own lack of control and bitterly acknowledging his defeat.

That damned book that was the cause of this entire mess. He should never have assumed Aurora would be shocked by the confessions of a courtesan. Honestly, his stupidity was mind boggling. She'd neatly snared him in a trap of his own making.

The moment the door shut and Aurora's carriage pulled away, Charles took himself in hand stroking the almost painful length of his cock. He spent himself in a handkerchief, grateful that Aurora had shut the door behind her.

Brought low by a girl in her second Season.

The situation could not continue. Aurora's absence was bound to be noticed, though certainly not by Miss Maplehurst who seemed to have completely abandoned her duties. Or one of his servants might gossip though they'd proved discreet in the past. Charles resolved to instruct Ropely to refuse her entrance when Lady Aurora attempted to call upon him again.

He shouldn't have underestimated her tenacity.

The following day Aurora appeared in Charles's study. She'd come through the kitchens after being denied entry by Ropely.

Charles hated that he was happy to see her, his hungry gaze running over Aurora's generous curves garbed in a dress of soft rose. Inhaling the scent of honeysuckle, Charles pasted a bored look on his face. "I am not receiving visitors today."

Aurora gave him a knowing look with no hint of apology. "Chapter two. Page eleven." She lifted her chin.

"This cannot continue, Aurora." It really could not. Charles was in danger of losing his mind over her. "I can't have you popping up uninvited. Or at all."

She held out the book, the page carefully marked. "The possibility of climaxing in such a situation intrigues me. I want to know if it is possible."

Charles opened the book.

Oh, sweet Jesus.

Considering the other things they'd done, the adoration of Aurora's breasts, suckling her nipples to bring about her release seemed tame. "I don't—"

Never taking her eyes from his, Aurora calmly undid the buttons stretching down the front of her dress. The fabric parted, exposing the pale cotton of her chemise and the shadow of her pert, taut nipples. "I'm not wearing a corset."

Charles attempted to compose himself. He'd dreamt of Aurora's naked breasts for some time, wondering how sensitive those delicious mounds might be given Aurora's inherently sensual nature. Her nipples were peaked and hard, practically begging for his mouth.

"Aurora, I insist you clothe yourself and—" The words froze on his lips as Aurora cupped both breasts, before reaching up to tug down the ribbon holding up her chemise.

Charles had seen a great many breasts. Nipples of all shapes and sizes. He was something of a rake, after all. But the sight of Aurora, with bits of lace teasing along those globes of flesh as the chemise fell from her shoulders, almost made him faint.

The entire visit lasted only half an hour. As it happened, Aurora and her breasts needed little coaxing from Charles. He suckled. Licked. Nibbled. Stroked. While Aurora made the most incredible sounds splayed across his lap once more. Her moans were muffled by biting into his shoulder.

Another failure at controlling his baser instincts. One of his best handkerchiefs ruined.

He almost prayed that Emerson would find out and beat him half to death.

In a desperate bid to maintain his sanity, Charles decided a trip to view Kenebruke's textile mill himself was in order. The trip would take the better part of a week, time enough to gain some perspective. He left no note and instructed Ropely that if Lady Aurora called, she was to be informed he would be out of town on business for some time.

Viewing the mill, walking the grounds, and noting the improvements that would need to be made kept Aurora out of his thoughts for the most part. He'd taken rooms at a nearby inn and even enjoyed the mild flirtation of a widow traveling through Manchester, though he didn't follow Mrs. Weathers back to her room as she suggested. The only thing he could think of was Aurora and what he should do about her.

As it turned out, Charles had to do nothing.

Upon his return from viewing the textile mill, a stack of correspondence and invitations awaited him, but not Lady Aurora Sinclair. Ropely informed Charles he had no female visitors at all while he was gone. The following day, Charles expected her to appear brandishing *The Bloom of the Rose.* He waited, somewhat impatiently, for her to appear.

She did not.

Charles poured a brandy and settled before the fire with a good book. He'd neglected his reading as of late except for *The Bloom of the Rose.* If Aurora had decided to cease this torment of him, so much the better. Possibly, she'd finally realized that her behavior was going to cause them both a great deal of trouble. Or maybe Aurora had learned enough from their time together and simply ended things on her own.

His chest hurt. Charles put it down to the excess of ham he'd had at breakfast, not the loss of Aurora.

Charles was vastly relieved. He could now go about pleasing widows and unhappily married women without a qualm. Enjoy the remainder of the Season without worrying over Aurora, who he meant to avoid like the plague. No one need ever know about his shocking lack of control.

Never once, while he sipped his brandy and read some dull tome on how best to dye wool, did Charles acknowledge how much he missed her.

CHAPTER THIRTEEN

AURORA STROLLED ABOUT the gardens behind Emerson House, a book clasped in one hand. Not *the* book, of course, but something more proper for her to read. No number of books, however, could keep the terrible hollowness over Worth at bay. He'd warned her that this was a dangerous game and Aurora hadn't listened. Now, she must admit defeat.

Plopping down in the grass, she lay back and stared up at the clouds in the sky, tossing the book aside. When she'd been a child at Dunnings, clouds had been Aurora's preferred entertainment. It cost nothing to envision goats, cows, sailing ships, and the like. Books, though, had been a luxury at Dunnings. The library, if one could call it such, boasted only a battered copy of the bible and a few unimportant novels.

A large cloud floated above her. If she squinted, the cloud resembled a pot of tea.

I'm fairly certain I'm in love with Worth.

It was the first time she'd allowed herself to think about her feelings since starting this entire affair. Three times she'd gone to him asking him to demonstrate an act from *The Bloom of the Rose*, all the while lying to him and herself. After the last episode, an erotic exploration of her breasts in which she'd climaxed from only the feel of his mouth on her nipple, Aurora came to the conclusion that she *did* have a wanton nature. At least when it came to Worth. Could she be wanton if she only wanted to experience that sort of pleasure with one man?

Aurora didn't think so. Thus, her conclusion that she loved Worth.

"He'll never love me back," she whispered into the breeze. "He deplores the idea of marriage, vowing never to wed. He's thirty. I think. Which I don't think is ancient. And rakish, though I don't believe him to be an immoral libertine."

Aurora didn't find Worth unsuitable, but *he* did, for the reasons she'd just named.

Closing her eyes, she stretched out her fingers in the grass, thinking of Worth's mouth on her own, his hands on her body, bringing about her pleasure with only the slightest touch. How simple it would be to simply corner her brother, Jordan, and relate to him that Worth had ruined her. Yes, she still had her virtue, but Aurora was far from innocent. Jordan would force Worth to wed her.

A tear slipped down her cheek.

Worth would never forgive her. Might even grow to detest the sight of her. She'd live her entire life with a man full of resentment, all directed at her.

"I want to wed for love," she whispered.

Then she could not wed Worth or force him to wed her.

There was a reason he'd kept her at arm's length and avoided Aurora as much as possible. Worth liked her a great deal. Desired her. But he didn't love Aurora and never would.

And Aurora *deserved* to be loved. She wanted a family of her own. Worth couldn't ever give her that.

The truth was a bitter pill to swallow.

"I won't see him anymore. I will return the book. My virtue is still intact. I can make a good match, either with Grisham or Healey." Falling in love with either man was impossible if she continued her relationship with Worth. Aurora believed in love. She was surrounded by it and refused to settle for anything less.

Aurora pressed a palm to the space above her heart, a choked sob coming from her lips. Worth could never be hers.

When Healey or Grisham called next, Aurora would be thrilled to see them. Her affections might be elsewhere, but each man deserved a fair chance to win her over. One day, Worth and her feelings for him would be nothing more than a wonderful memory. If she tried hard enough, Healy or Grisham could replace Worth in her affections. Aurora would need to encourage both of them, subtly, to steal a kiss. Now that she knew pleasure, it was important she find it again with someone who was not Charles Worthington.

Another sob left her.

"What a terrible, foolish mistake I've made." Aurora turned and cried into the grass, hating what she had to do and knowing there was no other choice.

CHAPTER FOURTEEN

C HARLES JOGGED UP the steps to Lord Kenebruke's London residence, intent upon the meeting he'd requested with the earl. Having viewed the textile mill, examined the the machinery and the operation personally, and made additional notes for Drew to review, it was time to restart the conversation with Kenebruke. Today was the first he'd had an opening on his calendar to speak to Kenebruke. Mr. Swift was making plans for an expansion of his ready-made clothing that would stretch over all of England. Drew had identified two more textile mills and an import company for Charles to assess. There was quite a bit of work to be done.

Business was also an excellent way to distract Charles from Aurora's absence in his life.

Her visits had not resumed. At first, Charles assumed Ropely was merely following directions and turning Aurora away, but that wasn't the case. Nor had Charles seen her at the two balls he'd attended earlier this week, both tedious affairs. He rode in Hyde Park, along the same path he'd found Aurora on that long ago day, but there was no sign of her. Charles did happen upon Patchahoo, Emerson's solicitor, who informed him Lord and Lady Emerson had gone to Rivercrest, the earl's country estate.

Only Lady Aurora and Miss Maplehurst remained in London. Which would have made visiting Charles that much easier had she wanted to see him. Which apparently, she did not.

"This is what I wanted. What I wished," he uttered under his breath. "It's for the best."

He kept waiting to be pleased by the turn of events.

Kenebruke's butler led him inside to the earl's study, where Kenebruke awaited him. Alone, thankfully. Mr. Healey and his idiotic suggestions were not in evidence. The meeting might actually provide the desired results.

"Mr. Healey isn't joining us today, my lord?" Charles said as he took a seat in a leather chair across from Kenebruke, and accepted a glass of brandy.

"No." Kenebruke's eyes twinkled. "Thomas had another appointment, one far more important than a dry discussion of textile mills. My nephew is courting a young lady. A rather lovely one. He's quite smitten, I think."

Good for Healey. If he'd found a woman to put up with his rather pompous behavior Charles was thrilled for him.

Kenebruke's brows drew together. "I confess, Mr. Worthington. I'm surprised you don't know, given your business partner is Andrew Sinclair."

Charles didn't so much as flinch as the words and their implication punched a hole through his chest. He took a slow breath, keeping only polite inquiry on his features, not the seething burst of jealousy echoing along his limbs. Aurora. Healey was courting Aurora. Smitten by her. And why wouldn't he be? She was magnificent. Charles knew firsthand.

He wondered what had happened to Grisham.

This is what I wanted.

"Sinclair mentioned something but I'm afraid I'm not overly invested in his sister's affairs."

What a terrible, horrible lie.

"Lady Aurora is a good match for my nephew, though she possesses a reckless streak. Not apparent during her first Season, but there, all the same. Likely due to her chaperone, Miss Maplehurst." Kenebruke's gentle laughter became a deep, hacking cough.

Charles recalled that day in the park. The carriage Miss

Maplehurst had disappeared into had belonged to Kenebruke.

Good for Miss Maplehurst.

Kenebruke continued to cough, so much so, he bent over the chair and Charles became concerned. "My lord?"

"I'm fine." Kenebruke waved him away, coughing a final time. "Just a cold. Now as to my nephew, it is well past time Thomas took a wife. I was already wed at his age. He hasn't shown a great deal of interest in any of the young ladies I've introduced him to, so I'm rather pleased he's so taken with Lady Aurora. Despite the notoriety of the Sinclair family, she is related to a duke, a rather powerful one. An association with Ware also brings one to Lord Curchon."

True enough. Curchon was Ware's uncle and an important minister in the Home Office. It was never a bad thing to be in favor with Curchon. "Two gentlemen whom you would always want on your side."

"Indeed, they are."

"I'm sure Emerson approves, as well as Miss Maplehurst."

"I assume so, but—" The lines around Kenebruke's mouth deepened. "I have not spoken directly to Miss Maplehurst about their courtship."

Odd. Charles was certain that Kenebruke and Miss Maplehurst were quite close. Lovers, in fact. At least that was the impression he'd taken from that day in the park. Perhaps the pair had a falling out.

The older man cleared his throat several times, swallowed his glass of brandy, then leaned over as another coughing fit struck him.

"My lord." Charles sat his own glass down. "Allow me to call for someone."

"No, it isn't necessary. I'll have the physician summoned as my nephew wishes, though it is only a mild complaint. My apologies, Mr. Worthington. I asked you to come today because we have much to discuss on the textile mill." Kenebruke leaned forward. "I needed my nephew gone for the day. His input is not required for this venture, though he believes it is."

Charles smiled. "I grew concerned you no longer wished to move forward with our partnership."

"Not at all." Kenebruke's eyes were sharp as they took in Worth. "What I wish to propose is a much broader partnership. What I did not disclose earlier, before I was sure we would get on, was that I've three additional properties. One of which makes only rope." He nodded.

"Only rope." Charles considered that carefully. Rope was vastly profitable. Kenebruke had more mills.

"But again, modernization is required, though not as extensively as the textile mill you viewed recently. I think an enterprise should be formed. Perhaps you'll even find other properties which might prove advantageous." Kenebruke smiled, coughed a bit more, and laid out the conditions of his proposal, all of which were generous.

"You don't mind if I do a bit more research, do you, my lord? It might take some time to put all of this together."

"I would expect it, Worthington, given your reputation. Thomas, though he tries his best, doesn't have a head for business. I want to be assured, one day when I am gone, that our partnership will provide him an excellent income with very little input from him, because *you* will be running it."

"Thank you for your confidence, my lord."

"It is well earned. I've asked my solicitor to draw up the proper contracts. You'll have them next week. Take your time to review the details. But I'm sure you'll be pleased."

"I don't doubt it."

Kenebruke's coughing started once more, wracking the older man until his entire body shook.

Charles took out his own handkerchief and handed it to the earl, relieved to see no telltale sign of blood upon the linen. Kenebruke only had a cold, not something more nefarious. He summoned Kenebruke's butler, who in turn sent for the elderly earl's valet to help him upstairs. Once the older man disappeared,

Charles took his leave, his concern for Kenebruke overshadowed by the knowledge that Healey was courting Aurora.

"It's for the best," he murmured for the hundredth time. Perhaps if Charles said so often enough, he might begin to believe it. It shouldn't matter that Healy was smitten with Aurora, his opinion on marriage or love wasn't going to change. Love held little illusion for Charles. There was nothing beautiful or romantic about it.

Damn you, Cecily.

His former betrothed was still dictating his actions even after all this time. Cecily had taught him about trust, mainly the breaking of it. Love wasn't beautiful. Or kind. Love was a torturous emotion. A manipulation. Marriage a mockery, whether made for status or some ridiculous romantic notion.

Not even for Aurora could Charles—

He pinched the bridge of his nose, took a deep breath, and attempted to concentrate on Kenebruke's proposal, which was likely to make Charles even wealthier. Drew would be ecstatic.

But though he was pleased, no overt joy filled him as Charles climbed into his waiting carriage. His thoughts were of Aurora.

Not of her coming apart in his arms, though that would stay with him forever, but the laughter in her eyes when she dared to kiss him. The way she pursed her lips when she played a hand of whist. The absolute horror of watching her toss a bowl at him from across the lawn. Her absolute bravery at marching into his home and demanding Charles give a demonstration from that blasted book.

He absently brushed his chest willing the ache there to stop.

Chapter Fifteen

Charles hopped out of his carriage as it arrived outside his home. He'd thought of little else but Aurora on the short drive, interspersed with bursts of possessiveness when considering she was likely smiling at Healey over tea at Emerson House.

He was greeted at the door by a resigned looking Ropely.

"You have a caller, sir. Lady Aurora awaits you in the study."

The jealousy from earlier returned. How dare she come to him after spending the day with Healey. "I see."

Coldness seeped into him, along with the sense Charles had been betrayed, though Aurora had done nothing wrong by encouraging Healey or being courted by him. Charles had made his position clear. Still, it felt very much—like Cecily.

Charles tamped down his rising anger. Aurora probably encouraged Healey to take liberties today or at least allowed him to steal a kiss. She knew well now how to find pleasure. Perhaps she'd found it with Healey. Why wouldn't she?

The pain stretched across his chest once more and he halted momentarily on the way to the drawing room.

If Aurora dared to brandish that bloody book at Charles and demand an "explanation" of a particular chapter, he would see her out himself.

He flung open the door of the drawing room. "Lady Aurora."

She was seated with her back to him, a glass clasped in one hand. Probably foxed once more. A convenient excuse for her behavior. Exactly as Cecily had done. Blaming the incident on having had too much to drink. Merely a slip.

He glared at Aurora. Charles was far wiser now. Well versed in betrayal.

"Are you drinking my brandy? A bit early, isn't it?" His tone was clipped.

Cecily had reeked of spirits. But she'd been far less composed.

Charles angrily pushed aside that memory, furious it kept resurfacing.

"Good day, Mr. Worthington." Aurora set down the glass and turned, her features schooled into bland politeness. "I've only had a sip. Stop trying to make me out as some sort of sot as you did the day of the garden party. Besides, today has been rather trying."

"Hasn't Healey put you in a better mood? Perhaps you read to him from *The Bloom of the Rose*. Or merely asked him to take a liberty or two. He must not have performed to your expectations given your presence here." Charles bit off the rest of his furious words. He sounded like a jealous suitor. Which he *absolutely* could not be.

Aurora looked taken aback. "You don't like Mr. Healey."

"My opinion isn't relevant."

"Given your behavior, Worth, I'd have to disagree."

Charles regarded her, the rush of ice filling his veins forcing out everything else.

"I find Healey to be unintelligent and overblown in matters of business. Which I am attempting to conduct with Lord Kenebruke if Healey would only stop inserting himself. Your involvement with him is a disappointment. I thought you possessed better taste."

Aurora swallowed, nodding slowly. "My affairs are my own, Worth. Whether you like Healey or not is irrelevant, because I like him. Quite a bit. I'm not sure why that matters to you."

Charles inhaled sharply at her tone. "He's a twit."

"A twit I might make a future with. You finally convinced me that our association was never meant to be long-lasting." A small laugh came from her. "And you need not fear I'll follow you about at a ball or a garden party. Or bother you further. I think you've taught me enough."

"I'm pleased to see you've come to your senses." Charles hated that she was so bloody composed.

"I'm sure you are most relieved." Aurora pulled the book from where it had sat hidden in her lap. She tossed it on the table before her. "I came to return your book."

He had never considered how much Aurora returning this stupid book to him might hurt. Or that knowing she would never visit him again left parts of him feeling shredded and torn. He should be glad of it. Thank her. The pain helped him refocus. Reminded him of Cecily.

"So you mean to wed Healey then?" The words were bland. Casual. As if he wasn't resisting the urge to kiss her senseless until she couldn't recall Healey.

"I'm not sure." She shrugged. "Possibly Grisham. I haven't yet decided between them."

The point being, no matter who she ended up choosing, it would not be Charles.

"Well, no matter on whom you decide," he said calmly. "I beg you to leave our association out of the conversation."

"You need not worry." Aurora came to her feet. "I wouldn't dare mention you. Good day Mr. Worthington. I can see myself out." Proud as any queen, she marched out of his drawing room and his life. Her heels sounded on the tiled foyer as Ropely saw her out.

Pouring himself a much larger glass of brandy, Charles took a seat on the settee, his hand touching the place where Aurora had been, the spot still warm and the air smelling of honeysuckle. The drawing room was completely still, empty and hollow without Aurora's presence.

Which only made Charles furious.

His drawing room, his *life*, were exactly as they should be.

Charles had been overly concerned, it seemed, with Aurora forming an attachment to him over the course of their association. But the opposite was true. She had managed to separate the pleasure they'd found together from her heart. Only Charles—

I am not attached to her.

His mind shouted the words before any other thought could be formed. It was merely the result of his ego, this terrible stinging sensation. Charles was usually the first to leave a dalliance or end an affair. Honestly, he couldn't call his association with Aurora either. What had it been then? Blackmail of sorts? Tutoring? The appeasement of her curiosity?

Charles snorted, nearly spilling his brandy.

This entire affair had been ridiculous in nature. Thank goodness no one had ever suspected. As amusing as it had been, Aurora was right to decline to visit further. Charles had no idea why he'd been so unsettled. She would go on to wed Healey— who should bloody well thank Charles and—

He swallowed down the rest of his brandy. Poured another. Finished it. Then decided to just place the bottle before him.

When next he saw Aurora because it was inevitable, they would once again be nothing more than familial acquaintances. Charles would probably be invited to her wedding to the tepid and uninspiring Healey. Or Grisham, that bloody prig. If she chose him.

His palm fell once more to the spot where Aurora had sat on the cushions. Her warmth was gone. Charles took several deep breaths. Forced himself to remember Cecily. Drank some more brandy.

It was some time later that Ropely found him, half-asleep on the settee.

CHAPTER SIXTEEN

AURORA GLANCED OVERHEAD at the sign in red lettering proclaiming she and Aunt Lottie had arrived at the apothecary shop. This apothecary she'd never visited, though Aurora had been to the small apothecary in Spittal many times after Mama had become ill at Dunnings.

The smell alone as she stepped inside reminded Aurora of all those useless herbs and potions Jordan spent precious coin on to help ease Mama's illness. But it had done little good. Mama had still died.

Her fingers dug into the sides of the door, foot hovering in the hair, unwilling to take another step.

Aunt Lottie took her hand, guessing at her reluctance. The older woman knew all about Dunnings and the cost that had been extracted. "There's no need for you to accompany me, Aurora. I can find what I need." A look of concern wrinkled her brow.

"When Mama fell ill, I traveled to Spittal nearly every day with Drew trying to find something that would ease her cough. Poultices. Tinctures. Nothing worked. I suppose I don't have much faith in such cures found within." She sent Aunt Lottie a weak smile. "I'll be fine in a moment."

"I'm sure you will be. Why don't you visit Tate's?" The bookseller stood three shops down from the apothecary. "Much more interesting to pore through those rows of books while I attend to business within this dusty place filled with dried herbs and lord knows what else. What I need will have to be mixed and may take some time."

Aurora gave the shop a wary look. She truly didn't want to leave Aunt Lottie who had been incredibly melancholy as of late. Kenebruke was the cause. "I don't want to leave you alone."

"Nonsense. I'm a solitary creature," her voice cracked just slightly, a sign of her distress. "I've been alone my entire life, Aurora. I can venture into an apothecary without your protection."

There were no more walks in the park with Aunt Lottie because Lord Kenebruke no longer appeared. The first time was shrugged off. But by the third occurrence, Aurora's heart had broken watching Aunt Lottie's tiny form on the bench, pretending to read. A note had been sent to Kenebruke, inquiring after his health, but received no reply. Nor did Kenebruke call again at Emerson House. The longer Kenebruke remained absent, the more quiet and distraught Aunt Lottie became.

What could possibly have happened?

"Retrieve me in an hour, Aurora. The sleeping draught should be ready by then. Plenty of time for you to browse and select something wonderful to read. Perhaps something a little scandalous. Go on. I know how you love books." A hint of smile appeared on Aunt Lottie's lips, though there were dark shadows beneath her eyes. She'd stopped walking in the park completely. Didn't sleep well. Ate barely enough to keep a bird alive. Most telling, she refused to discuss Kenebruke with Aurora. Wouldn't even mention his name. Aurora would have gone to Odessa with her concerns, but her sister-in-law, along with Jordan and little Douglas, had gone to Rivercrest for a few weeks. Only Aunt Lottie and Aurora inhabited Emerson House with Holly guarding them both like a giant mastiff.

If Aunt Lottie's mood didn't improve soon, she would write to Odessa.

"Are you sure?" Aurora looked at the apothecary shop, nose

wrinkling as something pungent escaped. She didn't want to abandon Aunt Lottie, especially when the older woman was clearly not herself. "I don't wish to leave you alone," she finally said.

"I have been alone a long time, Aurora." Deep sadness laced her words. "I can endure an hour at the apothecary."

"But—"

"Go," Aunt Lottie insisted.

"I won't be gone long. I promise." Aurora took the older woman's fingers before releasing Aunt Lottie's hand for the short walk to Tate's. The Emerson carriage was parked between the two shops, driver and footman waiting should she or Aunt Lottie require any assistance.

A hint of citrus floated through the air toward her from a passing gentleman making the breath catch in her throat. He smelled like Worth. Likely used the same shaving soap. Aurora's chest constricted. She'd done an excellent job of keeping him from her thoughts since she'd returned *The Bloom of the Rose.* Worth hadn't called at Emerson House, not that she'd expected him to. At the theater a few days ago, Aurora had caught the briefest glimpse of him sitting beside Lady Duggins in one of the private boxes. The widow's entire form was tilted toward Worth as she whispered something in his ear.

Aurora straightened her spine and walked confidently into Tate's.

At first, the anger and hurt that Worth had let her go so easily without so much as a protest had Aurora moping about. She wanted to believe his dislike of Healey was jealousy, but his mood wasn't about her at all. Merely business with Kenebruke.

In all fairness, Worth had done exactly as Aurora asked. She'd demanded he demonstrate pleasure and satisfy her curiosity, which he had. No other promises were made. Aurora wanted to believe she and Worth would remain friends.

Friends. Could she honestly just remain a distant familial acquaintance of Charles Worthington?

Thank goodness she'd returned that bloody book before anyone saw her reading it. *The Bloom of the Rose.* What a ridiculous name for an erotic book.

Where had Worth found such a thing? Certainly not Tate's. Although she supposed, given his reputation, he could have picked it up anywhere. Oddly enough the shelves of his study and drawing room weren't filled with anything remotely erotic in nature. For a supposed rake, Worth had a rather boring collection of books. Crop rotation. Shipping routes. Geological surveys. Scores of pamphlets on financial matters and banking, none of which looked the least appealing. Worth's reading material was so varied that if a random stranger peeked at the shelves, they'd have no idea what he was really interested in. But Aurora supposed that was what made Worth so good at identifying investments. Hester, Drew's wife, once said that Worth surprised her by relating a string of facts about honeybees and the profitability of keeping hives. He'd made several suggestions to improve the selling of her honey, all of which she'd taken.

"Drat," she whispered entering Tate's. Here she was, once more obsessing over Worth instead of other, more pertinent matters. What had occurred between Aunt Lottie and Lord Kenebruke for one. It was only that Aurora missed him, far more than she wished.

"I merely need an excellent book to take my attention from Worth. Something with no hint of romance or physical relations."

Worth on his knees, his mouth between her thighs flashed before her eyes. Aurora halted, took a deep breath, and forced her feet forward.

"A travel book," she hissed under her breath. "Or perhaps something on deportment. That should help me sleep if nothing else."

Aurora tried to envision sitting on Grisham's lap. Or Healey's. But could not. That was rather the problem, wasn't it? The idea of doing any of the acts described in *The Bloom of the Rose* with either gentleman left Aurora cold. She only wanted to do those things with…Worth.

Stop thinking about him.

Healey confessed a great deal of affection for her, Grisham less so. But both gentlemen were far better for her than Worth. She must give them a chance. She wasn't trying hard enough.

Sliding down one aisle, Aurora's skirts whispered along the crowded shelves as she trailed a finger over the leather-clad spines, still attempting to force Worth from her thoughts. Incredibly difficult. Missing him had become something of a daily habit, one Aurora struggled to break. Inhaling the scent of leather, paper, and ink, she smiled at the neat rows of books.

Such extravagance. Books.

When one struggled to find enough to eat, books were a great luxury. Dunnings had been devoid of even the smallest comfort. The Sinclairs barely had enough money to purchase enough coal to see them through the winter, let alone stock a library.

Ironic, considering Dunnings sat on an enormous deposit of coal.

Knowing Aurora's love of reading, Jordan would scrape together what little extra coin he could, whatever was left after selling a pig or if he'd won a fight at the tavern in Spittal, just so he could buy some battered novel for her from a passing peddler. She'd cried each time Jordan presented her with a tattered book, clasping it to her chest in absolute joy.

Aurora still had each one of the books Jordan had purchased for her, refusing to leave them at Dunnings when the Sinclairs returned to London. She cherished each one, no matter how stained the pages or how moth-eaten the covers.

"Lady Aurora."

She came to a halt before her favorite section, one full of questionable romantic novels. None of them were horribly scandalous, in Aurora's opinion, but neither were they considered appropriate for an unwed young lady. And the very last place she'd ever expect to see the gentleman before her.

"Why, Mr. Healey. Whatever are you doing here?" Aurora tried to keep the surprise from her words. After a flurry of carriage rides through the park and a pleasant trip to Gunter's where they'd sampled ices, Aurora hadn't seen Healey much the last week, though he'd sent her flowers. It occurred to her, as she looked up into his handsome features, that while she liked Healey a great deal, she'd barely noticed his absence. Unlike the lack of Worth which pricked at her every day.

Perhaps I merely prefer Grisham.

Unfortunately, Aurora didn't miss him either.

"If you recall, I adore Tate's much as you do, my lady." Healey's gaze lingered over her bosom discreetly before clearing his throat.

"I remember your love of books, Mr. Healey, but you never mentioned you cared for novels of a romantic nature."

His lips pursed as if tasting something not to his liking. "I'm on an errand for my uncle, Lord Kenebruke."

"I wasn't aware of his liking for such things. How is Lord Kenebruke?" Perhaps she could find out why he hadn't called on Aunt Lottie or met her in the park.

"Ill, I'm afraid to say, and unable to leave his bed. A terrible cough settled in his chest, though he is now, thankfully, on the mend." Concern lit his eyes. "I'm in no hurry to inherit, I don't mind telling you."

"I'm sorry to hear of it." Kenebruke had been ill. Did Aunt Lottie know?

"The clerk directed me to this section, but—" Two tiny dots of pink appeared on his cheeks. "I must have misunderstood his direction. I assumed there would be books on military campaigns." He looked at a scrap of paper in his hand.

Aurora giggled. "Not in this section, Mr. Healey. I thought you were here on purpose."

"No." Mr. Healey wedged himself against the shelf, attempting to hide the row of lurid romances from Aurora's view. Which was ridiculous. "I'm—merely in the wrong aisle. I'm sure of it. My uncle couldn't possibly wish a book from this area."

Aurora bit her lip to keep from laughing at his obvious discomfort. This section was entirely devoted to juicy romantic tales, but the most shocking tomes were hidden on the other side. Thank goodness he hadn't ventured any further. Poor Healey was definitely a prig, though not nearly as bad as Grisham, who would have burst into flames at only seeing the titles Mr. Healey was so desperately trying to shield Aurora from.

"Perhaps I can offer assistance, Mr. Healey, or at least help you find what you're looking for. I daresay I am as familiar with Tate's as Mr. Stevens."

"Mr. Stevens?"

"The clerk." She nodded to the front of the store. "You mentioned military battles and the like. Roman? Greek? Or—"

"My uncle asked for a specific title." He peered at the slip of paper once more. *The Adventures of Captain Duncan.*"

Aurora tried not to burst into a fit of giggles and risk offending Mr. Healey. "*The Adventures of Captain Duncan?* Are you certain?"

"The clerk, Mr. Stevens as you say, gave me an odd look when I asked for it by name and sent me to this area of the shop. But he must not have heard me correctly. I can't imagine the memoirs of a sea captain would be in this section."

"Rather scandalous reading," Aurora said. "Captain Duncan, I mean."

Aurora had read *The Adventures of Captain Duncan.* As had Aunt Lottie. The main character, Captain Duncan, was a bold calvary soldier, who battled his way across the Continent while carrying on affairs with dozens of women. Romantic. Sensational. Lots of swords, of both kinds.

"Not military history, then." A puff of resignation left Healey. He appeared quite put out. "I thought as much. I beg your apology, my lady, for even mentioning such tripe to you. I can see you are distressed. Forgive me."

Good Lord. The books weren't *that* wicked. Kenebruke must have chuckled to himself at sending his overly starched nephew in search of the novel.

"I've read *The Adventures of Captain Duncan*," Aurora admitted.

Healey's eyes widened. "You have?"

"Very enjoyable. Highly entertaining. Only a bit scandalous." She reached around Healey and pulled *Captain Duncan* from the shelf behind him. "He'll enjoy it a great deal. I promise." She handed the book to him, wanting to roll her eyes at the effort he made not to touch her fingers. At least he hadn't collapsed in a fit of horror at having known Aurora had read the book. "You made no mention of Lord Kenebruke's illness when last you called, Mr. Healey. Or left a note with the flowers you sent. You left me wondering over your absence." Not entirely the truth because she hadn't honestly missed him. A fact Aurora meant to examine later. "I would have sent Lord Kenebruke a wish for a speedy recovery had I known."

Healey made a disgruntled sound as he took *Captain Duncan* from her outstretched fingers. "You've actually read this, my lady?"

"I have." Aurora didn't look away. "Why did you not inform me your uncle was ill?"

He continued to study the book in his hands, running the tips of his fingers over the title. Healey kept his eyes averted from hers. "After our visit to Gunter's, I arrived home to find him already with the physician," he started. "My uncle overexerted himself in a business meeting, one he should have allowed me to oversee given how unwell he has been of late." Healey's jaw hardened. "I have been by his side ever since. I—didn't want to worry you needlessly. My apologies," he finally glanced up from the book in his hand, "for not sending word to you."

Healey *should* have sent a note. Better yet, he should have called on Aunt Lottie and informed her of Kenebruke's illness. He had to be aware of the relationship between the earl and Aurora's chaperone, or at least, suspected the pair were friends. Aunt

Lottie's mood would vastly improve were she to know that Kenebruke wasn't purposefully ignoring her but had instead been ill.

"My uncle is recovering slowly," Healey continued. "Last night, I allowed him a brandy and to finally leave his bed for dinner. I fear he is not used to being ill. He's a poor patient. I've been handling his correspondence and business affairs while he recovers. *The Adventures of Captain Duncan* was recommended to him by a friend, though I can't imagine anyone at his club did so."

It could only have been Aunt Lottie.

"Miss Maplehurst will be most relieved to know Lord Kenebruke is feeling better," Aurora ventured. "But quite distressed to find Lord Kenebruke has been ill and she was unaware." She dared to admonish him.

Had Healey deliberately kept word of Kenebruke's illness from them or was it merely an oversight on his part?

Healey's upper lip twitched, unable to completely stop the sneer trying to form at the mention of Aunt Lottie. Nor did he make any excuses. Aurora thought that very telling.

"I must take my leave, my lady." The ugly look faded to be replaced with his usual shy smile. "My uncle will be attempting to leave his bed and I cannot allow it without at least some supervision. He still coughs quite a bit. And I must still visit the apothecary on his behalf to purchase a syrup for his cough." He bowed to her.

Good. Healey would be sure to bump into Aunt Lottie at the apothecary. He would not be able to ignore her without being outwardly rude or creating a small scene. The news about Kenebruke would come better from him, at any rate.

"I bid you good day, Mr. Healey. Again, please convey my best wishes to Lord Kenebruke."

"I shall." He hesitated. "Now that my uncle is better, I'll be in attendance at the Travers' ball." The unspoken question hung in the air.

"As will I," Aurora answered.

"May I be so bold as to request my dance now?" His tone had grown warm and accommodating, which made it easy to forget his stuffy behavior. Healey tended to be overly polite and conscious of every impropriety, but he also possessed a dry wit. He could be quite amusing. Aurora was certain a passionate soul beat beneath that properly tied cravat. She need only force it to the surface.

"You may." Aurora allowed him to take her hand and nodded politely. She waited until waiting until Healey made his way to the clerk's desk to pay for his uncle's book before turning back to the shelf before her. Though she liked Healey, his attitude toward Aunt Lottie was troubling. As was his near obsessive need to watch his uncle's every move. Perhaps she was making more of Healey's devotion to his uncle. Or maybe his behavior was more indicative of a controlling streak.

That wouldn't bode well for a future together.

Aurora resumed her perusal of the books, humming as she considered Healey and then Grisham. One of them must be induced to at least steal a kiss. Now having known arousal and the resulting pleasure, Aurora wouldn't settle for less in a husband.

Carefully, she stepped to the other side of the shelf where much more wickedness abounded in the form of scandalous works and penny dreadfuls. Aurora quite enjoyed a good penny dreadful. Odessa had introduced her to such shocking reading matter after marrying Jordan, along with criminal broadsides, which Aurora hadn't even known existed. Criminal broadsides tended to be much more gruesome.

"The Highwayman's Revenge." Aurora chewed on her lip in thought. Was she in the mood for pistols and coach robbing? She put the slim volume back down. No, she was not. No pirates either.

Spring Heeled Jack. Her eyes widened at the cover which had a macabre figure with claws hovering over the top of a building, about to leap on the unsuspecting young couple below.

Perfect.

"You've rather shocking tastes in literature," a voice drawled through the books lining the shelf. "Though given your recent reading material, I can't say that I'm surprised."

Aurora's pulse ticked up, the rhythm becoming unsteady. A whiff of citrus and leather caught in her nostrils along with a hint of orange.

This was entirely unfair. First her thoughts, now he'd appeared before her.

She was *trying* to forget him.

Yes, but that isn't going well.

A pair of sparkling eyes the color of sapphires peered at Aurora between two tomes clad in red leather.

"Mr. Worthington."

Aurora steadied herself as he came around the bookshelf. Leaning against a stack of criminal broadsides, Worth studied her with an amused smile. Bloody breathtaking as always. Not so much as a small cut from shaving to mar his perfection. Her entire body stirred in reaction to his appearance.

Entirely, absolutely, unfair.

"In the flesh," he murmured.

The wickedness of his reply sent a ripples along her skin. A gentle caress spread low in her belly before darting between her thighs.

Worth didn't seem angry. There was no chilliness in the curve of his lips. No dismissal in his tone as there had been after Aurora returned *The Bloom of the Rose.*

If anything, Worth was downright seductive as he stared at her in the dusty confines of Tate's.

CHAPTER SEVENTEEN

C HARLES HAD DONE an an excellent job of staying hidden while that pompous, self-important idiot Healey preened over Aurora. Stuttering and blushing like some virgin because he'd stumbled upon a collection of romantic novels. If Healey had any idea of the sort of reading material Aurora genuinely enjoyed, Kenebruke's nephew would swoon.

The initial dislike of Healey had only intensified since Lord Kenebruke had unfortunately fallen ill. The contracts from the solicitor laying out the terms of the new business venture Charles and the earl had discussed, never arrived. The modernization of the textile mill had come to a stop. Kenebruke's solicitor had made the mistake of consulting Healey about the documents—a tragedy for all involved because Healey, who was a bloody idiot, insisted due to his uncle's illness Kenebruke had been unable to review the contracts thoroughly.

Healey decided that he must do so himself.

He dithered, putting at risk the agreement while pretending financial acumen Healey didn't possess. Desperate, Charles had tried to send Kenebruke a note, but Healey returned it stating his uncle could not be bothered at the moment, as he was ill, and all future correspondence should be sent directly to Healey.

There were many reasons for his dislike of Healey. But the sight of that twit eyeing Aurora's bosom had Charles *furious*. He'd wanted to take Healey's strictly tied cravat and strangle him with it.

Charles was *jealous*.

The emotion was foreign to him, having not felt it for ages. No, that wasn't entirely true. The same, annoying, jagging sensation had been present the night Aurora gave him back the book when she mentioned Healey. Or any other man.

He'd spent the nights since her final visit drinking brandy and allowing Lady Duggins to dangle from his arm. Lady Duggins, bless her. She'd tried so desperately to garner his interest. But Charles couldn't even bring himself to kiss her.

Had that staid prick Healey seen Aurora's face when she climaxed? The soft pink glow that would sink into her cheeks making her appear as if she were blooming?

That sight belonged to Charles and *only* him.

He'd spent the last quarter hour envisioning how best to punch Healey in the nose without getting blood on himself.

Brandy usually helped dull such possessive thoughts, but unfortunately there wasn't any at hand. Tate's didn't offer a full sideboard to patrons. Seeing Aurora, so bloody fetching in yet another shade of blue—she had to have some sense it was his favorite color—Charles was having a great deal of difficulty remembering exactly *why* he vowed to never wed. Why he preferred an indulgent lifestyle full of meaningless affairs. Avoided the romantic involvement. Couldn't afford to compromise his heart again.

Healey finally walked away saving Charles from causing them all undue embarrassment.

Aurora had done this to him. Brandishing the book—

I gave her the book.

Threatening to toss herself at any gentleman in the vicinity out of carnal curiosity if Charles didn't capitulate. Kissing him in the maze.

You kissed her back.

But mostly for making Charles remember—*Cecily*.

Damn.

The tip of Aurora's finger caressed the spine of one very questionable book as he regarded her, one which should have been hidden behind the counter at Tate's. No young lady should even know about such a volume nor even touch it. Most would shudder as if they'd come across a leper. Or faint.

Lady Hamerly's Baseborn Lover.

But not Aurora who possessed an incredibly reckless nature. An inherent sinfulness. Lacking any sort of shyness on sexual matters as proven by her proposal to Charles.

Aurora on his lap, grinding against his cock came to mind.

But she was also intelligent. Witty. Deeply sensual. Possessed the unlikely ability to grow cabbages. Drew had related how his sister had managed to supplement the larder at Dunnings by growing whatever would take root at that desolate estate. Cabbages. Carrots. Some beets. When an army of worms had invaded her small, pathetic garden, Aurora had wept, terrified her family would starve unless she could fix matters. She'd gone to great lengths to protect the cabbage, resorting to collecting the worms off the leaves each morning and disposing of them in the kitchen fire.

Aurora was much more than a beautiful creature gowned in silk and only interested in gossip and balls. He'd tried so hard to put her into that box, but she was nothing like Cecily.

"*Lady Hamerly's Baseborn Lover.* A true delight, I'm sure," he quipped.

"Poorly written." Aurora nodded to the books clasped beneath his arm. "Have you found something here you fancy, Mr. Worthington?"

You. I fancy you.

Difficult to admit but entirely true.

Charles held up the first book. "*Secrets of Crop Rotation.*" Showed her the second. "*Arable Farming Methods.*"

"Fascinating, I'm sure."

"There is property in Lincolnshire I'm convinced would be a good investment for Drew and Hester. Blackbird Heath should be growing more than potatoes and cabbages. Was that Mr. Healey I caught sight of?"

"He was picking up a book for Lord Kenebruke, who has been ill," she said. "Has he really disrupted your dealings with his uncle so terribly that you cannot at least mute your dislike of him?"

Charles shrugged not willing to admit that his animosity of Healey had more now to do with her than Kenebruke. "He pretends knowledge he doesn't have, treating Kenebruke as if he were addled and incapable of making a decision, which is not the case. But I do know the earl has been ill."

"He is a bit overprotective given Kenebruke's age; I'll agree." Her brow wrinkled slightly. "I do not know what sort of venture you've proposed to Kenebruke, nor do I need to, but have you considered Mr. Healey doesn't understand how the situation is beneficial? To both his uncle and the estate." She cocked her head. "And ultimately Mr. Healey?"

"Impossible. How could he not."

"Sometimes a person cannot see what is clear before them," her voice grew quiet. "They are far too close and thus blinded. You might point out, *gently*, that he is likely to reap the rewards of your business venture, far more and much longer than Lord Kenebruke."

Kenebruke had mentioned the same. And if it wasn't for Aurora, perhaps Charles would have looked far kinder on the earl's nephew.

"Mr. Healey isn't as intelligent as you, Worth." She gave him a rueful smile. "And you are both aware of it. Mr. Healey much more so than you. It probably makes him antagonistic toward your business venture with his uncle. He's trying to prove himself. And no, Mr. Healey would never stoop to discussing business matters with me. A young lady." She snorted derisively. "He's far too polite."

"I will consider your advice. It's rather sound. Perhaps Healey should discuss business matters with you. I know I would."

A wry smile pulled at her lips as her fingers lazily caressed one of the tomes in front of her. "Good." Aurora stepped into a patch of sunlight, the chestnut of her hair glittering with strands of red-gold.

Charles drew in a slow, agonizing breath, considering that slender hand on him and not the books. He dreamt of her touch when he lay in bed alone at night. Recalled the sensation of her skin. Wanted her beside him.

He found Aurora to be the most beautiful of creatures, not only in appearance, but because of her strength. Her determination. She'd survived Dunnings and the taint of her family's name to become—well, the sort of young lady who propositioned a rake like him.

"I can still taste you on my tongue," the whisper came from the depths of his soul, rolling from his lips before he could stop. "Feel your softness clutching my fingers. Hear you moaning my name."

A sound, part distress, mostly desire, came from her. "Worth."

Stepping closer before he could think better of it and flee, Charles caged her lush form along the wall. Lowering his chin, the tip of his nose glided along the edge of her cheek. "Page nine," he murmured. "I think chapter one. How to arouse with barely a touch."

"I've returned the book." Aurora's lips parted softly. "You could be making that up."

"But I'm not." Charles very carefully inhaled along the side of Aurora's neck, lips grazing the honeysuckle-scented skin. She smelled so luscious, so wonderfully feminine, and soft. He moved along the modest neckline of her dress, barely touching the lace, his tongue flicking out to taste the barely visible curve of her breast.

"Your tongue," she breathed, arching her back. "Does that constitute touch?"

He lifted his chin, delving into the sensitive spot beneath

Aurora's left ear, where a tiny bit of jet dangled from the lobe. "Possibly."

Her breathing grew strained, the mounds of her breasts pressing against her bodice, stretching the fabric.

Taking the jet between his teeth, Worth tugged gently before using his tongue to trace the outline of her ear.

Aurora's fingers clutched at his coat.

"No. Palms against the wall." His voice was rough. "Barely a touch. My touch." Charles didn't care that they were in Tate's, where anyone could come across them. He had the inclination to raise her skirts, search beneath those bloody petticoats while she moaned.

"I miss you." The words came tumbling from her as he nipped at the lobe of her ear. "I know I should not. That you only indulged me and sought to keep me from ruination."

Charles worshipped that plump bit of flesh, toying with it as if he were still buried between her thighs.

"You've never allowed me to give you pleasure, Worth," she panted. "As if not doing so was some sort of penance. Yours, not mine."

Charles stopped the worship of her earlobe and pressed his forehead to hers, overcome by Aurora. She knew him, in a way no one else did. She always had. Perhaps that was part of why Charles found her to be so terrifying.

"You do give me pleasure, Aurora Sinclair," he whispered, placing one hand on her neck. His thumb caressed the pulse beating in her throat. Lips lowering, he claimed her mouth with a groan of satisfaction. Aurora tasted of lemon and honey. Of sensual dreams and promises.

Charles pushed her further against the shelf, covering her smaller form with his own.

She surrendered beneath him, parting her lips, small, perfect little tongue tracing the inside of his mouth.

Cupping one breast in his palm, he squeezed, listening to her sigh. Full and rounded with small, pink nipples. He could see her breasts in his mind, no matter the layers of silk and cotton. The tips hard as diamonds. Incredibly sensitive. He could adore them for hours. They were that perfect.

Aurora whimpered, pushing her hips to catch at the growing hardness in his trousers. She nipped at his mouth. One hand clutched at his shoulder. The other, his backside.

God, she's perfection.

Charles wasn't sure of what exactly he meant to do about Aurora. Brandy and longing only got him so far in his thinking. At the moment, his mind wasn't working correctly. All he could comprehend was the feel of her in his arms and the twitch of his cock.

The click of heels sounded on the floor just on the other side of the bookcase that hid them. Skirts rustled announcing the impending interruption.

Charles broke away from Aurora, quickly covering her mouth with his palm. She sagged along the bookshelf, watching him with heavy-lidded eyes.

"Someone's coming."

CHAPTER EIGHTEEN

Aurora blinked, barely hearing Worth through the haze of
desire echoing along her skin. Warmth slid away as he
jerked back, pulled his hand from her mouth and rapidly walked
down the aisle in the opposite direction. He disappeared
immediately behind another section deeper inside Tate's before
Aurora even came completely to her senses. Somewhat dazed
and horribly aroused, she turned her eyes back to the shelf and
Lady Hamerly's Baseborn Lover.

What had just happened?

She had returned the book to Worth with the assurance she
would not bother him further. Ended their relationship, if one
could call it that. He hadn't protested. Now, just when Aurora
had resolved to stop her ridiculous longing and force herself to
fall in love with another man, Worth appeared and kissed her
senseless.

Aurora pressed a palm to her midsection, trying to quell the
taste and feel of Worth. And a great deal of confusion over his
behavior. She took several deep breaths. Composed herself. No
good would come if whoever lurked on the other side of the shelf
caught sight of her swollen lips and the heated flush along her
skin.

Glancing down at her bodice, she adjusted the lace.
Smoothed her skirts. Finally, assured all was in order, she peeked
through the books before her.

Only a sliver of the aisle was visible until a voluptuous form in silk strutted into sight, stopping abruptly on the other side of the bookshelf, like some hunting dog spotting a poor fox. An overpowering floral scent filled the air.

Lady Bryant.

"Worthington," the sugary tone cooed, echoing down the aisle before moving forward with determination. "Is that you cowering in a stack of dusty books? It is you. I was surprised to see you here, at Tate's, of all places." She disappeared, her voice fading into the depths of the bookseller.

Aurora turned to the window, trying to make out her watery reflection. She looked appropriate. Not so much as a hair out of place. No sign of near ravishment. Nodding to herself, she slipped into the aisle and headed in the direction of the clerk, Mr. Stevens. With any luck, she could escape the bookseller without being noticed by Lady Bryant.

"Lady Aurora, did you find anything to interest you?" The clerk's cheery voice boomed far louder than she found necessary.

Aurora cringed but managed a smile. "Not today, I'm afraid." She took a quick glance toward the back of Tate's.

Lady Bryant's head poked around a bookshelf. Her narrowed stare focused on Aurora.

"Well, then," Stevens continued, "we've a new shipment coming in a week from today. I'm sure there'll be something to interest you, my lady. Shall I send word to Emerson House when it arrives?"

"Yes. That would be lovely. Good day to you, Mr. Stevens."

Aurora walked sedately out of Tate's as if she hadn't been kissed and groped, willingly, against a stack of scandalous books. Difficult not to sprint away from the curious, discerning gaze of Lady Bryant.

Had she seen Aurora and Worth?

They'd hardly been quiet. Lady Bryant could have observed them silently before making her presence known.

She tripped on a loose cobblestone and quickly righted.

Lady Bryant *had* seen Aurora and Aunt Lottie leaving the maze at Lady Berriwell's garden party. At the time, she hadn't given it much thought. She'd obviously been waiting for Worth to appear. But—

She hurried over to the apothecary just as Aunt Lottie strolled out, a smile on her face and a small package clasped in her hands. "There you are, Aurora. I was just about to seek you out at Tate's." Glancing down at Aurora's empty arms, she said, "I expected an entire stack of books. Did one of the footmen already put them in the carriage?"

"No," Aurora said, linking their arms. "I didn't find anything of interest." A bit of warmth crawled up her cheeks. Or rather she had, but it wasn't a book.

"You're a bit flushed." Aunt Lottie raised a brow and turned toward Tate's. "Did you find something scandalous? Please don't tell me you were reading penny dreadfuls. I should never have allowed Odessa to introduce such things to you. Or was it a novel and you are afraid to purchase it?" Her brows raised. "Tell me the title and I'll march over and retrieve it for you. Every soul in London already knows I'm improper. I'm reading it first." Her eyes twinkled. "And we won't tell Emerson, will we?"

Aunt Lottie's mood was *greatly* improved. Mr. Healey must have informed her about Kenebruke's illness.

"No. I told you there was little of interest today, though Mr. Stevens assured me another shipment of books will arrive next week." Aurora steered the older woman toward the waiting carriage. Getting away from Tate's would be in Aurora's best interests. The last thing she wished was Worth or Lady Bryant to find her outside. Not in her current state. She waved at one of the footmen to open up the carriage door.

"Trollop," Aunt Lottie muttered as the footman bowed at their approach.

"What?"

"Oh, not you, dear." Aunt Lottie tilted her chin toward Tate's. "That *dreadful* Lady Bryant. She's over there preening like some flirtatious peacock. I've had my share of dalliances, but I've always been discreet."

Not entirely true. But Aurora didn't correct her.

"But that woman," Aunt Lottie shook her head, "is a viper. Discretion is not in her vocabulary. She hops from man to man at every house party she attends. Is it any wonder that Lord Bryant has taken up with Lady Pearse? Malicious gossip. Much like her cousin, Lady Longwood." Aunt Lottie nodded. "Except that Lady Longwood isn't a trollop. I can't fathom any gentleman ever wanted to dally with her. Might be why she's always in such a terrible mood."

Oh. Dear. "Lady Longwood?"

"*Distant* relation. But birds of a feather." Aunt Lottie gave a small laugh. "Which is appropriate given the feathers Lady Longwood likes to wear. Atrocious things. I can't recall how they are related, exactly. Doesn't matter. Best to give her wide berth, as we did at the Berriwell garden party."

"Why didn't you mention their connection when we saw Lady Bryant at the party?" There was no sign of Worth outside of Tate's. Either he was still inside, or he'd left by by the back door where the bookseller took deliveries. She didn't want to see Worth just now, especially after Aunt Lottie's revelation.

Aunt Lottie gave a tiny shrug. "Did I not? I suppose in the excitement of seeing Kenebruke I forgot." She turned toward the carriage, just as Worth exited Tate's.

Lady Bryant hurried to him, taking his arm.

Worth's former paramour—well, Aurora reasoned with sickening dread—Lady Bryant might *still* be his paramour. She was also the cousin of Lady Longwood. The very woman responsible for nearly everything terrible in Aurora's life. She'd pushed Bentley to banish them all to Dunnings. Mama had *died* because of Dunnings. Tamsin had nearly been destroyed by that woman's vile nature. Drew was Worth's closest friend. His business partner.

How could he?

Aurora gave one last glance at Worth. How was it possible Worth didn't make the connection between the one lady in all of London whose sole purpose seemed to be the destruction of the Sinclairs? Or did Worth simply not care? For a time, inside Tate's, Aurora would have said Worth felt something for her. Maybe not love, exactly. But the seed of it. That kiss had given her hope.

Her stomach pitched unpleasantly.

The truth was that Aurora had no way to know whether Worth was still involved with Lady Bryant. There had been no understanding between them. He was well within his rights to satisfy his needs elsewhere, no matter how much the thought pained her.

Aurora only hadn't thought—

Another wave of nausea rolled through her. She pressed a palm against her stomach and turned her chin, not willing to observe Worth and Lady Bryant a moment longer.

"What is it, Aurora?"

"Breakfast might not have agreed with me," she said without so much as a tremble despite her distress. "The eggs were undercooked. Nothing more."

"I'll inform Mrs. Cherry when we return." Aunt Lottie gave her a skeptical look.

One of the footmen hurried forward to assist Aurora inside the carriage.

"Oh, I forgot to mention, Mr. Healey was at the apothecary." Aunt Lottie leaned forward. "Lord Kenebruke has been ill." That beautiful glow filled her lovely features once more. "A terrible cough has sent him to bed. So weak he has been unable to even answer correspondence. Had I known I would have been at his side."

"I thought it must be something of the sort," Aurora settled next to her. "That he was ill or had to unexpectedly depart London for business."

"In truth, I—" She waved her hand. "Well, it no longer signifies. Only that I feel terrible for Kenebruke. At the very least I could have read to him. I don't imagine Mr. Healey does." She nodded. "His eyesight is quite awful. You must encourage him to see an oculist, Aurora. I had to march right up to him before he saw me. Mr. Healey was so intent on relaying his order to the apothecary he barely spared me a glance until I raised my voice. He apologized profusely, of course."

"I'm sure he did." Aurora clasped her hands and glanced out the window as the carriage rolled forward.

"I think he feels terrible about causing me any distress, which is probably why he didn't send word Kenebruke was ill. Very thoughtful. He's such a gentleman. You could do far worse."

Aurora stayed silent. The apothecary wasn't large. It would be impossible not to see Aunt Lottie unless you were intent on avoiding her. Which Healey must have been.

"I am undecided on Mr. Healey." Much more so now than she'd ever been. Had he seen the note Aunt Lottie sent to Kenebruke asking why he no longer rode through the park and merely tossed it in the fire? Such suspicions, when she liked Healey, were unwelcome.

But not nearly as unwelcome at the sight of Worth and Lady Bryant.

Aurora avoided thinking about seeing them together in the maze, instead choosing to only consider what had come after, the kiss with Worth in the grass. But she hadn't wanted to think about Worth and Lady Bryant as lovers. She still didn't.

"Well, Mr. Healey is not undecided where you are concerned, Aurora. He will be at the Travers' ball. As will you."

"So he told me." At Aunt Lottie's look she said. "I saw Mr. Healey at Tate's. He was purchasing a book for Lord Kenebruke to keep him entertained while he recovers. We only spoke in passing, but he did ask me to save him a dance." Her fingertips touched her mouth, the feel of Worth still on her lips. She didn't want to believe he might also be involved with Lady Bryant.

"*The Adventures of Captain Duncan.*" Aunt Lottie clapped her hands. "I told Kenebruke he'd enjoy the story. More so were I to read it to him. I didn't mention that to Mr. Healy."

Aurora leaned back against the leather seats. "Probably for the best, Aunt Lottie."

CHAPTER NINETEEN

L ADY BRYANT HOVERED at the door of Tate's, watching Charles like some sort of well-dressed vulture while he calmly paid for his purchases. When she'd caught up with him, at the far corner of the bookseller, she'd had a questioning gleam in her eyes. He'd had to turn his body, holding the books at his waist, to hide the significant tenting of his trousers. Not even the coat he wore could disguise the state Charles was in.

The clerk at the front, announcing Aurora's presence, didn't help matters.

Hildie exited Tate's first, and he had hopes she'd go on her way to find another victim, only to find her waiting for him outside. What was she even doing at a bookseller? Hildie deplored reading, claiming it to be a tedious pastime. She never bought gifts for her husband, whom she detested. The only explanation was that she'd seen Charles going inside, which meant it likely Hildie had also seen him and Aurora together.

He tried to avoid her upon exiting, but this time, Hildie clutched at his arm. Resigned to her presence for the time being because he was unable to shake her off, Charles looked up to see Aurora and Miss Maplehurst climbing into the waiting Emerson carriage.

His heart jumped in her direction. Against his will and in spite of everything he'd vowed years ago.

Never *again*. Not after Cecily broke him into dozens of pieces. Aurora wasn't Cecily, rationally he knew that. The two were nothing alike. Even so, there was still an entire list of reasons why Charles should avoid Aurora even if he couldn't remember them all now.

Maybe he didn't want to.

"You haven't heard a word I've said, Worthington."

Hildie. God, he'd almost forgotten she and her nauseating perfume were still standing beside him, clinging like some sort of overzealous Pomeranian. He wanted to kick at her. What had he once liked about her? Charles had once thought her beautiful and she wanted very little from him, only a good tupping. That had been the attraction. The absolute certainty no real attachment would ever form between them.

"Apologies, my lady. I fear my mind is elsewhere. A business matter I've yet to finalize."

"I asked if you are going to apologize for leaving me at that dreadful garden party. I had to ride home with Lord Rollings. He's a *dreadful* bore. I nearly jumped out of the carriage to find some relief."

"He was once your lover," Charles countered not bothering to apologize. Hildie had probably had her skirts around her ears the entire trip back to London.

"So were you," she snapped back. "But you've not called upon me."

"Was I supposed to?"

Hildie glared up at him. "I was turned away from your door when I called."

"We never had any formal arrangement. No understanding other than when bored we might amuse each other." Charles inclined his head anxious to be away from her. "A way to pass the time. Never more than a convenience."

"You enjoyed yourself," she sniffed.

"As did you, Hildie. I'm not sure why you are so put out. You are married, or have you forgotten?" Why didn't she just go away?

"Oh yes, sometimes I forget. Bryant is far more interested in that cow, Lady Pearse."

Charles didn't blame him. Lady Pearse was vastly preferable to Hildie.

"Is your lack of interest in me because of Lady Aurora Sinclair?"

Charles stilled. "Excuse me?"

She rolled her eyes. "*Really*, Worthington. I saw her come out of the maze with that elderly harlot who serves as her chaperone. Hair in disarray. Cheeks pink. I'll assume that was your doing. When she calls, you receive her." Hildie's tone was bitter. "Tell me, do you look at books together, as you were doing today?"

Charles kept his features bland. "Are you watching my house, Hildie? How desperate you are for attention."

A blush stained Hildie's cheeks and neck. She finally released his arm. "Lady Aurora isn't the least discreet. But what can you expect, she's barely more than a child." A laugh burst from her. "I thought your tastes more refined."

His fingers tightened on the wrapped package containing his books. If he hit her over the head would anyone take note? Or care? "Refined? Goodness, I took *you* as a lover, didn't I?"

The blush darkened to crimson. "Tucked back on a bookshelf at Tate's." Her lips curled. "Her mother was a trollop and her sister little better, though Lady Tamsin managed to snare a duke. One who pays little attention to anything else but insects," she trilled. "Some think him simpleminded."

"He's an entomologist," Charles bit out. "Should I write that down so you may look up the word?"

"When I mentioned having seen Lady Aurora at Berriwell's garden party to my cousin, drifting aimlessly about, *brazenly* eyeing poor Lord Grisham, well, I heard all about your little tart's pedigree. I confess, I knew the Sinclairs were laden in scandal, but I hadn't imagined just how tainted they were."

"Your cousin?" Honestly, he had rarely conversed with Hildie, preferring to keep their relationship to the physical and nothing else. He couldn't recall who she was related to in society.

Her lips rippled in an ugly manner. "Lady Longwood. I could have sworn I'd mentioned her."

She hadn't. Not once. Charles wasn't so self-absorbed that he wouldn't recall the woman who'd nearly destroyed the family of his closest friend.

"You knew Andrew Sinclair was my business partner," he stated quietly. "And never mentioned your relationship to Lady Longwood?"

"I'm sure I mentioned her." A smug smile graced her lips. "Oh, that's right. Sinclair is your business partner."

Bitch.

"Perhaps I attempted to blot it out. Andrew Sinclair lives on a *farm* in Lincolnshire. Mucking about with his low-bred wife. The daughter of the town sot. Sinclair is probably fleecing that little backwater of what coin they possess. Good lord, Emerson was a pig farmer and is wed to Angus Whitehall's daughter." Hildie snorted. "Brother of Viscount Worthington or not, you'll be judged by the company you keep."

Charles didn't doubt that Hildie and Lady Longwood would make sure of it.

"Good day, Lady Bryant." He turned his back on her, determined not to give into his anger in the middle of the square where anyone could see them. Where Aurora could see them.

"Poor Worthington. Still broken hearted over sweet Cecily. Pity. Goodness, what a scandal. My cousin recalls it quite clearly. No wonder your brother keeps his distance."

He swung back to Hildie, looming over her until she took a step back.

"You're a horrible, vicious creature." His smile was wide, despite the ice of his words. "Truth be told, you're a bore, Hildie. Entirely predictable. Pathetic. Posing in front of a statue and begging me to lick your quim." He gave an ugly laugh. "Such desperation. I wonder what the gossips would make of that?"

"You wouldn't dare, Worthington."

"Sour grapes, Hildie. That's what everyone will say once they know I've refused your advances. How you crave me so much, you hide in wait outside my home to watch my comings and goings."

Hildie sputtered.

"I'll laugh, of course, and say it wasn't unexpected. After all, you did chase me into Tate's today. Begging me for an assignation. But do go conspire with Lady Longwood who everyone knows is unhinged by her hatred of Lord Emerson. Tell anyone who will listen you think the Duke of Ware is simple and weak. See what happens."

Her lips tightened. "You will regret those words, Worthington."

"Not half as much as knowing you, Hildie. I can't believe I once thought you amusing."

She made a horrible, strangled sound. If they hadn't been in public, Hildie might well have screamed.

Charles rolled his shoulders and strolled off, books clutched tightly in one arm. He'd never once considered hitting a woman in his life, but Hildie could certainly be the first if he didn't get away from her.

CHAPTER TWENTY

AUNT LOTTIE TOOK a chair among the other matrons clustered on this side of the Travers' ballroom, just to the right of the Dowager Duchess of Ware. The two women stared each other down, when neither flinched, both sniffed and then exchanged a polite greeting.

Aurora released the breath she'd been holding. Meetings between Aunt Lottie and the dowager duchess could often be unpredictable. Thinly veiled insults were hurled, often covered in compliments. References to the past that no one could quite understand. Spilled tea. An upturned plate of scones. Comments on each other's clothing.

Very much like two schoolgirls.

Their mutual animosity stretched back at least four decades according to Ware. Odessa claimed that the hostility started when each walked into the same ball wearing a gown of identical style and color. Both women had once patronized the same modiste in their youth. The only notable difference between the two gowns had been the cut of the bodice. Aunt Lottie's, as expected, had a much more indecent neckline. The entire ballroom that night had erupted in conjecture before either of them took to the dance floor.

Aunt Lottie found the entire incident amusing. She still did. The dowager duchess claimed utter humiliation.

The blame was fixed on the modiste, who soon left London

for France.

How two gowns and an uncreative modiste had caused such a feud was anyone's guess. Aurora assumed a gentleman was at the core of their dislike. Possibly both women had been rivals for his affection. It was no secret that the former Duke of Ware had been uninterested in his duchess. Aunt Lottie had never wed and remained a spinster.

It all made perfect sense.

Aurora tapped her foot in time to the music, imagining what the two older women had looked like as young, carefree girls, scorning each other across a dance floor in matching gowns. What a sight that must have been.

Content to watch the proceedings from her place between both ladies, Aurora observed the swirl of dancing couples. Lord Grisham had already received his dance earlier, merely reinforcing Aurora's tepid feelings for him. A pity that the earl was dull as dishwater. Not even the wide breadth of his shoulders and his athletic build could overcome such an obstacle. Grisham could barely carry on a conversation beyond the weather and horses, neither of which Aurora had the least interest in.

Such a shame, because he was quite attractive.

Grisham had politely conversed with the dowager duchess and Aunt Lottie, earning smiles from both before promising Aurora to return at some point.

No matter how handsome Grisham was in his formal wear, Aurora wasn't sad to see him depart. Once they'd exhausted the topic of whether rain would fall tomorrow followed by a description of a gelding he meant to purchase from Tattersalls.

Aurora hoped to see Mr. Healy tonight, not only for his own sake, but because Lord Kenebruke might also be in attendance. Aunt Lottie's mood had lifted dramatically after seeing Healey at the apothecary and learning that Kenebruke's absence was due to a bad cough. She had smiled for the remainder of the week, sending off two notes to Kenebruke wishing him a speedy recovery.

Both went unanswered. Just as before.

Aurora suspected Mr. Healey's interference. She did not voice her thoughts to Aunt Lottie.

Her plan, when Healey appeared, was to confront him herself. There was much to like about Kenebruke's nephew and Aurora wished to give him the benefit of the doubt. He could be overly polite. A tad pompous. Controlling, even. But she had also caught glimpses of his sense of humor. He was thoughtful. Kind. Enjoyed reading and books as she did. Best of all, Healey was transparent in his admiration for Aurora. She didn't have to wonder at his feelings for her.

Unlike Worth who blew hot and cold depending on the day.

Upon returning from Tate's that day, Aurora had spent the remainder of the afternoon writing out a series of letters to Worth, all of which ended torn up and tossed into the fire. She wanted an explanation for the passionate, intoxicating kiss they'd shared at the bookseller. A kiss that should never have happened because Aurora had returned the book. Worth had made his position clear. There was also the matter of Lady Bryant. Was he really so bloody obtuse he didn't realize his paramour's cousin was Lady Longwood?

Aurora took a deep breath. Clasped her hands before her and kept her gaze on the couples dancing.

The longer she considered Worth, the more incensed at his actions she became. Aurora had stopped short of throwing on her cloak, hailing a hack, and showing up at Worth's door to demand answers. Ropely, his butler, would admit her to the drawing room without blinking an eye. After all, he had before, discreetly shutting the door behind him.

Poor Ropely. Aurora did wonder what Worth's butler thought of her. Had he heard her screaming out her pleasure into the cushions of the settee?

But she hadn't gone to Worth that day, or any day since. Charging down the stairs, Aurora had made it only as far as the drawing room before realizing the absolute stupidity of her actions. Nothing would be served by arriving at Worth's home, unescorted. Tossing off her cloak, she had gone straight to the sideboard, refusing to look at the portrait of her parents smiling above the fireplace as they would certainly disapprove, and poured a healthy glass of Irish whiskey.

Aurora had sat before the fire for a length of time, sipping whiskey, considering how brazenly she'd pursued Worth without any shame. Insisting he was merely a tutor of sorts. Rather embarrassing, when it came down to it. What right did Aurora have to question him after the tone she had set?

"I don't," she said, her thoughts returning to the Travers' ballroom. Lifting her head, she looked scanned the room, absently looking for Mr. Healey. Her perusal was stopped by a pair of eyes, gleaming with malicious intent. The spray of feathers spilling wildly atop the lady's coiffure gave away her identity. Pale yellow garbed her stark, angular form and when combined with the headdress of feathers gave Aurora the impression she was being stared down by an overly large chicken.

Lady Longwood snapped her fan, flinty eyes never leaving Aurora even as she bent to whisper something to the woman beside her.

Lady Bryant.

Aurora was unsurprised at their staring or the smug tilt to Lady Bryant's crimson lips. Likely they were dissecting Aurora's character, her origins, and the fit of her gown. Aurora had never spoken to Lady Longwood directly save when she'd been a child. The day the Sinclairs were banished to Dunnings she'd leaned over a terrified Aurora and whispered, *Deadly Sin*. Though only a child, she remembered the utter contempt Lady Longwood had shown Mama. The only other encounter she'd had with the dowager viscountess had been at a modiste's shop when the Sinclairs had returned to London.

Aurora lifted her chin in challenge to Lady Longwood.

Come here and say those things.

Lady Longwood didn't dare.

Not with Ware's formidable mother looming over Aurora, like a lioness protecting her cub.

If there was another lady in society more terrifying than the Dowager Duchess of Ware, Aurora had yet to meet her. The dowager duchess was feared in London society. One word from her and all of London might give you the cut direct. She did not tolerate fools or vile gossips.

Aurora found her to be a fierce and loyal protector. Much like her son. And despite Aunt Lottie claiming she didn't have one, the dowager's prickly exterior hid a warm and loving heart.

"I never did care for Lady Bryant," the dowager drawled from Aurora's left. "She's intolerable. Goodness, I've seen doxies with more modesty."

"At last, we can agree," Aunt Lottie said from Aurora's right. "I pity Lord Bryant for his poor choices."

"Lady Bryant attempted to call upon me once." The side of the dowager's mouth lifted. "But I was not at home. I cannot fathom why she thought I would find her of any interest."

"I doubt you would have been entertained, Your Grace. Given the company she keeps." Aunt Lottie tilted her chin at Lady Longwood. "Wine after a time turns to vinegar, though I hadn't considered it to be true of people."

"Lady Longwood's pursuit of Lord Jeffries has gone awry." A ghost of a smile pulled at the dowager's mouth. "Pity, since Lord Longwood has nearly bankrupted his estate. As dumb as his father, or so I've heard."

"Isn't Lord Curchon closely acquainted with Jeffries?" Aunt Lottie gave the dowager a sideways look.

"My brother is acquainted with a great many gentlemen." The dowager gave a careless roll of her shoulders, but her smile widened just a bit.

Aurora didn't react to the information other than to feel a gleam of satisfaction at Lady Longwood's circumstances. How fitting, since Lady Longwood had once banished the Sinclairs to suffer in poverty. Aurora had little pity for her or her terrible son.

"Oh, the irony." Aunt Lottie shook her head. "Lady Longwood has two daughters. I'm sure either one would take her in."

"Yes, but their husbands will not." The dowager laughed softly. "She should have cautioned Longwood against spending so lavishly. But she seems to believe herself immune from creditors. The duns beat at his door nearly every day."

"She is starting to resemble a bird of some sort, don't you agree, Your Grace?" Aunt Lottie discreetly ran her gaze across the ballroom, looking for Kenebruke, no doubt. "One that squawks about ruining everything."

"A feral pigeon, perhaps?" the dowager asked. "Destructive things. Always roosting where they aren't wanted. I am always so pleased when my cats bring one down."

"Can cats be coaxed to take down a person?" Aunt Lottie mused.

"Unfortunately, no. They are difficult creatures at best and have no master."

Aurora was enjoying this conversation immensely. She didn't think Aunt Lottie and the dowager truly disliked each other. At least not anymore.

"A chicken," she interjected. "It's the feathers Lady Longwood insists on wearing in her hair along with the yellow gown. Or perhaps one of those mythical winged creatures who attempt to claw at your eyes."

"Harpies." Aunt Lottie smiled. "An apt comparison."

The dowager wrinkled her lips in disapproval, but her eyes twinkled. "A young lady of good breeding should not speak so, Aurora. I fear Miss Maplehurst is a lost cause."

Aunt Lottie nodded. "I am in complete agreement."

"I'm a Sinclair, Your Grace." Aurora patted the dowager's hand. "My breeding has always been in question and fodder for the gossips. But I will heed your advice, nonetheless."

"As you should," the dowager's imperious tone commanded.

Aurora liked Ware's mother a great deal. She was more than a bit bossy. Vastly superior. Somewhat obsessed with cats. Very much like Ware, though his tastes ran more to insects. And much to the surprise of everyone in London, she adored and protected her new daughter, the former Tamsin Sinclair, shredding those who dared to cast a disparaging sniff in the new Duchess of Ware's direction. She had embraced all of Aurora's family, just as Ware had done.

"Lord Grisham is acceptable in my opinion," she murmured to Aurora. "Attractive, wealthy and from good family." The dowager didn't so much as lift her eyes from the ballroom floor where the dancers swirled about. "Well-mannered. But I fear you do not find him as appealing as I do."

"I think him a lovely gentleman, Your Grace."

"But?"

"He's boring, Your Grace." Aunt Lottie interjected. "I've had tea with Grisham. Goes on about the weather, which is to be expected. But then he settles in on horses. Nothing but horses."

"Well, Grisham breeds them on his estate, so I understand his interest. Fine horses, I may add." The dowager raised a brow.

"We've nothing in common, Your Grace." Aurora gave her an apologetic look. "I don't think we'd suit."

"I see. Perhaps over time?"

"No, Your Grace."

"Hmm. And what of Mr. Healey? He'll be an earl one day." She watched Aunt Lottie from beneath her lashes. "Kenebruke," she paused, "won't live forever."

Aunt Lottie glared at her. "Nor will you."

The dowager laughed softly. "Goodness, Charlotte. I'm only stating the obvious. Consider our ages." She huffed. "At least he's no longer married."

Aurora had been correct. The feud between the dowager and Aunt Lottie *did* have to do with a man. Given the conversation, all signs pointed to Kenebruke. She was about to ask, as innocently as possible, how the dowager came to be acquainted with Lord Kenebruke, when a honey-blonde shock of hair appeared in the crowd atop a lean, elegant figure.

Worth.

His chin tilted in Aurora's direction almost as if he'd heard her say his name. Magnificent in his dark evening clothes, the stark attire a perfect foil for his aristocratic beauty. He easily put every other gentleman in the ballroom to shame, at least in Aurora's opinion. They regarded each other across the ballroom for scant moments before Worth disappeared, heading in the direction of the room set aside for cards.

Well, that was disappointing. Did she not deserve the pretense of a polite greeting? Manners would demand he'd at least greet Aunt Lottie and the dowager duchess. But she supposed it best if she and Worth didn't speak to each other.

Lady Bryant's eyes followed Worth before she detached from Lady Longwood. Purposefully, she strolled in the same direction as Worth.

Aurora kept herself still, refusing to allow the sight of Lady Bryant sauntering after Worth to bother her.

A wave of nausea struck her.

"Charles Worthington. Such a rogue," the dowager said lightly. "Entirely too charming for his own good. Hardly a gentleman, though his brother the viscount, most certainly is. But eye catching all the same. Like a jewel set in gold catching the sun. Brilliant, I'm told by Ware."

"That is my understanding as well, Your Grace," Aurora answered. "I doubt Drew would have become his business partner otherwise."

A tiny sound came from Aunt Lottie. She pressed a hand to her throat as if distressed by something. "I—"

"Is something amiss, Aunt Lottie?" Aurora immediately went to her side.

"Not at all, dear." Her hand fell back to her side. "It is only that the terrible punch we've been served, and the heat of the ballroom has caused my temples to ache. I should—find a quiet spot to rest for a moment. Gather my wits once more."

"I completely agree. I've often considered you witless." The dowager waved a gloved hand. "If you follow that corridor, Charlotte, you'll find a small parlor. The interior is painted a horrid shade of green. Much like a gown I once wore many years ago. I never really cared for that gown, Charlotte. Not then," she gave Aunt Lottie a meaningful look, "or later. I don't believe I've ever told you. At any rate, despite the atrocious hue, the parlor is quite private. I doubt you'd be disturbed, were you to lie down and rest. At our age, Charlotte," the dowager punctuated each word, "one should not put off such things."

Aurora looked between them. The two were not speaking of a gown.

"I also had the misfortune of a gown in that same terrible shade of green. Too many flounces and ribbons. I daresay, I don't even care for green. A momentary madness overtook me else I would never have—" her eyes caught those of the dowager, "worn it. I discarded the gown as soon as I found out how—poorly it was made." Aunt Lottie bobbed politely. "Please excuse me, Your Grace. Lady Aurora." She walked swiftly away in the direction of the corridor the dowager had pointed out, weaving around the dance floor and disappeared from view.

Aurora took a deep breath. "Was it Kenebruke?"

"Who?"

"The gown," Aurora asked. "I think it must be Lord Kenebruke you are speaking of."

The dowager gave her a shrewd look of approval. "Clever girl. It was not Kenebruke. Though I did happen to spy him across the ballroom a short time ago, leaning heavily on his cane." She looked up at Aurora. "Fell from a horse. Leg didn't heal properly. At any rate, he'll need to rest. Our hostess will have directed him to that terribly decorated parlor. She's terribly proud of the décor for some unknown reason." She gave a shiver of disgust.

"Why?" Aurora's heart swelled with affection for Ware's mother.

"Well, for one thing, my eyesight is much better than Charlotte's. She's been squinting the entire evening which is incredibly distracting. Had I not pointed out his whereabouts, Kenebruke might well have left soon due to his leg."

"Who was the gown, Your Grace? I knew it had to be a gentleman."

"None of your affair." The dowager rapped Aurora's knuckles with her fan. "Don't be impertinent. Now let us discuss Mr. Charles Worthington."

Aurora turned back to the dancing. Better not to face the dowager after such a question. "What of him? Worthington is a friend of the family. My brother's business partner. He taught me cards and bowls."

And pleasure. A great deal of it.

"The color on your cheeks at the mention of his name suggests a deeper acquaintance though you attempt to hide it." She sighed. "I would caution you, Aurora, that Worth is a *confirmed* bachelor, one with a somewhat poor reputation."

"You mean he's a rake. I am aware. Who could not be?" Aurora's fingers curled into her skirts thinking of the way Lady Bryant had so boldly followed him.

"Not an entirely terrible one," her voice softened. "But his intentions toward you," she held up a hand before Aurora could protest, "could not possibly be honorable."

"What would cause you to say so?" Aurora spun about. "He's always behaved in an honorable fashion toward me," she lied.

"Cecily Millstone," the dowager intoned. "They were to wed, Cecily and Worthington. You were all still at Dunnings," her lips tightened, "when the scandal broke. Worthington behaved like a cad. Ending the betrothal without explanation. Humiliating Cecily. He took up with a string of women. Cecily's father was furious at the slight done his family and nearly called Worthington out. There were rumors, you see, that Worthington had already ruined her."

Aurora swallowed down the lump in her throat. "How terrible."

"Not the actions of an honorable gentleman, Aurora. I do not wish you to endure the same fate."

"You need not worry, Your Grace." Her mind reeled from the dowager's words. Worth was an unrepentant bachelor. He'd never disagreed when Aurora claimed he'd be a terrible husband.

"Cecily eventually wed a marquess. She was beautiful enough that her future husband chose to overlook the fact she was," the dowager leaned forward, "*damaged goods*. You do not wish to be damaged goods, Aurora."

"I don't think any young lady would wish such a thing, Your Grace."

Aurora kept trying to believe Worth was more than a rake. That he cared for her. And she supposed he did, on some level. He had warned her away, more than once. But in her heart, Aurora hoped—

He'd offer for me.

Now, after hearing about Cecily Millstone, Aurora knew how truly foolish she'd been. There had never been any chance of Worth deciding differently. Hadn't she known it? Wasn't that why she'd ended things with him? Her heart *and* body had been compromised. And yes, had things continued, Aurora would have allowed him to ruin her.

I would have begged him to do so.

And that bloody confusing kiss at Tate's? Just another example of his flirtatious behavior. For all Aurora knew, he followed Lady Bryant home immediately after. And even after all of that, knowing well what their relationship truly was, Aurora *still* allowed that tiny seed of hope inside her to flourish.

"I fear I've distressed you," the dowager said quietly.

"Not at all, Your Grace. I am not blind to Worthington's faults. Nor have I mistaken his kindness to me as anything other than mild affection. The sort one has for a friend's younger sister. He would make a terrible husband. When Drew was wed, Worth declared quite adamantly that he never wished the same for himself."

Aurora's heart tightened painfully.

"I'm glad to hear it." The dowager took her hand. "Though I grant you, Worthington is splendid. More than enough to turn a young lady's head. Now, let us discuss Mr. Healey."

"Mr. Healey." Aurora didn't want to think about him at present. Healey would one day be an earl. He was solid. A bit priggish, but Aurora could fix that. Most importantly, she and Healey had a great deal in common. Mostly books, but she felt safe in assuming there would be other things if she took the time to look. And while Healey didn't inspire Aurora in exactly the same manner as Worth, she thought with enough kissing and direction, he would.

"Mr. Healey comes from good family. He's smitten with you. Healey will be stalwart and loyal I think. You could do worse."

There was the matter of his dislike of Aunt Lottie, but perhaps she had misinterpreted his actions. Maybe it was merely a case of him being overly protective of Kenebruke. If she ended up wed to Healey he would have to accept Aunt Lottie's relationship with his uncle because Aurora would insist upon it.

"I will consider his proposal when it is offered."

"Good." The dowager waved her hand. "Because he approaches."

Aurora composed her features, shutting away the anger at Worth and the pain of her misguided heart, and smiled at Mr. Healey.

CHAPTER TWENTY-ONE

C HARLES DUCKED INTO the room put aside for cards, sliding about the tables, nodding to those he knew. He'd caught sight of Hildie dogging his steps as he made his way down the hall. Rotten luck to be spotted by her and Lady Longwood the second he entered the ballroom. He had an urgent need to speak to Aurora, particularly after what happened at Tate's, though Charles had no idea what he'd say. Only that things were not finished between them.

Aurora was stunning in a gown of rose silk this evening. Chestnut hair piled into a mound of curls atop her head and studded with brilliants. A goddess come to life in the Travers' ballroom. The sight of her beckoned Charles like some bloody siren despite the unwelcome glance she gave him.

Charles didn't dare approach Aurora, not with Miss Maplehurst and the austere Dowager Duchess of Ware on either side. Nor could he while Hildie and Lady Longwood watched him so carefully. Those two bitter harridans would make much of him greeting Aurora and draw far too much attention. Gossip was sure to follow.

Hildie was obviously out for blood, his in particular, but Lady Longwood wanted nothing more than to sink her claws deep into Aurora. Worth was aware of his reputation. Knew what the cost would be to Aurora if their association was not assumed to be innocent. Keeping his distance tonight would be wise when there was more than one pair of eyes aimed in his direction.

So Charles had kept his distance from Aurora, deciding to play cards for a time. But Hildie had followed. Now he was fleeing from her as discreetly as possible. That's when he heard the whisper of her name.

Cecily.

Charles halted momentarily at hearing Cecily mentioned, though Hildie was bearing down on him.

On rare occasions at events such as this, Cecily Millstone's name floated about. But not often enough to make Charles avoid going out in society, not anymore. Years ago, he'd allowed himself to be branded as a dishonorable rake because it was vastly preferable to the truth. He allowed Cecily to go about weeping that Charles had cruelly discarded her. She was ruined. Everyone knew it.

In all fairness, Charles did bed her, but he'd trusted that Cecily would be his wife.

He could not, however, take credit for her ruination.

Trust. Once gone, it was impossible to repair. Especially in Cecily's case.

Aurora is not Cecily.

Charles made his way to the other side of the room, ducked through a doorway, and found himself once more in the hall. Moving toward the ballroom, he was relieved to not see Hildie behind him.

Aurora and Cecily were as different as two women could be. Cecily had been willowy with barely a bosom to speak of. Auburn haired. Undeniably cultured and beautiful. The epitome of the perfect lady.

She'd never spent a day digging in the dirt flicking worms off a cabbage.

Aurora was generous in both form and heart. Witty. Intelligent. Deeply sensual. And she held her whiskey exceedingly well. Cecily displayed no such talent, blaming spirits for a variety of her misdeeds.

A gentleman pushed past Charles, jolting him out of his musings. The elbow purposefully nudged Charles in the back with an elbow without apology. He turned to say a word to this rudely impolite gentleman and stopped.

Healey.

A rude word was not required.

Lord Kenebruke had called on Charles just yesterday, solicitor at his side, apologizing profusely for any misunderstandings while he'd been ill. The contracts had been signed. Their business venture for the mills, complete. Given the dressing down Healey likely received from his uncle, Charles should be glad Healey hadn't pushed him harder. Healey had been shut out of the situation. As he should have been from the start.

Charles watched Healey stomp off. Kenebruke's nephew was making a beeline for Aurora.

Possessiveness pinched at him. Another unwanted emotion he hadn't felt since Cecily. He didn't want Healey touching Aurora or even speaking to her. The urge to punch the younger man in the nose had him forming a fist. How satisfying it would be to break the bridge. Blacken his eye. Watch Healey's blood drip all over Lord Travers's fancy ballroom.

It took so little to turn a gentleman into a savage, didn't it?

He melted into an alcove, just before the entrance of the ballroom, watching happily as Lady Bryant passed, paused and searched the crowd, likely for him, and then moved on. He sunk into the darkness further, when Healey, his fingers firmly wrapped around Aurora's elbow, escorted her toward the dance floor. She was laughing, her cheeks alight with color, shining like a jewel as Healey whirled her around.

Kenebruke's nephew had the personality of a beet if he possessed any one at all. He was far too reserved for Aurora. She'd fall asleep from boredom if he bedded her.

A growl sounded inside Charles.

Nevertheless, Aurora smiled up at Healey. They made a striking couple. Even Charles had to admit it. Aurora would be a countess when Healey inherited from his uncle. But he doubted she cared about such things.

Unlike Cecily.

Charles had no idea how ambitious his former betrothed was until she fucked Viscount Worthington, his father.

The ugliness of that memory flooded Charles in an instant, no matter how he tried to shut it back away. Hide it all so that Charles never had to look at it again. But this business with Aurora had that old bitterness and pain leeching out of him again, seeping through his fine clothing, and reminding Charles that in the end, he hadn't been enough for Cecily.

He might never be enough for anyone.

How often had Charles examined that day? Replayed those moments in his father's study over and over. The betrayal by two of the people Charles had loved most in the world—

Glancing down at the floor, he struggled to regain his composure. Thinking too much on Cecily always did this to Charles because he recalled how his heart had beat only for her. How pathetically romantic he'd been.

How he would never allow himself to be such a bloody idiot again.

He looked up once more to see Aurora spinning about in Healey's arms, more lovely than a sunrise on a spring morning. Had Healey held her in his lap and heard the sounds Aurora made as she climaxed? Had she told him about *The Bloom of the Rose*? About the older, slightly debauched rake she adored?

His chest squeezed tight.

He hoped Aurora still adored him. Charles had taken that for granted. Too stupid to see—

No, he didn't think Healey knew Aurora at all.

Healey swung her expertly about as he watched. Kenebruke's nephew was a good dancer. If Aurora wed Healey, Charles would be treated to this sight until he could no longer bear to look.

Strange, he'd seen Cecily dance with the Marquess of Dutton and not once had he wanted to tackle Dutton on a ballroom floor and beat him senseless.

When the dance ended, Healey did not return Aurora to the care of the dowager duchess. Nor Miss Maplehurst, of course. As usual, Aurora's chaperone had abandoned her duties. Which allowed Healey to lead Aurora to the terrace doors open to the much cooler evening air.

Charles followed.

CHAPTER TWENTY-TWO

"**M**UCH BETTER, DON'T you agree? I confess I nearly fainted while we danced, the air was so warm." Aurora released Healey's arm and slid away from him. The dancing had made her heated, and an unpleasant dampness pooled beneath her arms and gathered at her temples. Once the dance ended she'd coaxed Healey into taking her outside, mainly because he'd immediately suggested finding Lord Kenebruke so he could check on his uncle. Suspecting Aunt Lottie was already assessing Kenebruke's condition in that hideously decorated parlor, Aurora thought it best to distract Healey with escorting her out to the terrace.

The terrace was far quieter than the ballroom had been but not devoid of other guests. Couples and small groups were clustered about, most intent on avoiding the lanterns spilling light along the terrace. Others wandered about the gardens, if the burst of giggles Aurora could make out were any indication.

"It is a splendid idea." Healy's teeth shone in the spill of light as they walked, side by side, passing a lamp.

Aurora thought Healey quite handsome tonight in his formal wear. Healey's lips, in particular, could be considered inviting. Not as full or sensual as Worth's but—

Stop this instant.

"Quite a few moths about tonight." Healey batted one away. "Terrible things."

"*Arctia caja.*" Aurora thought her Latin was approving. Ware would be pleased.

Healey's brows drew together. "I beg your pardon?"

"The moths." She nodded at the pair circling the lamp. "*Arctia caja* is the name in Latin. A tiger moth. You may recall, my sister's husband, the duke, studies insects. Ware has taught me everything I know about moths and beetles." Aurora grinned at him, wondering if Healey would be amused or horrified that she'd helped Ware prepare specimens. "He's a well-known entomologist and spent several years studying and collecting moths. His research is now on display at the Entomological Society. He's quite famous amongst academics."

"I'm not familiar," Healey gave her a rueful smile. "But I think the duke far more intelligent than I. Despite the fact that if I see an ant or a beetle, I am more likely to stomp on it than collect it."

"I won't tell Ware. He would be quite cross with you."

Healey's hand dropped from her elbow as he faced her. "I— would like to speak freely, if I may, Lady Aurora."

"That sounds ominous, Mr. Healey."

He pulled her into an area full of shadows. The scent of the garden, a combination of flowers sifted in her nostrils. It was a lovely night. The sort meant for stolen kisses. Healey might not approve, but Aurora was determined to steal a kiss if he didn't do so first. Not terrible, in her opinion, to kiss a man she was considering marriage to, though if the wrong person came upon them, Aurora would be considered compromised. Or her wanton nature confirmed.

She sunk further into the darkness.

Healey didn't arouse her as Worth did, but Aurora reasoned it was unlikely any other man would. She was attracted to Healey and that was a good start. Given enough time, Aurora was certain she could love Healey. It wouldn't be the wild, passionate tearing at her heart that she felt for Worth, but more steady and solid in nature. Less painful in nature, but still beautiful.

The story of Cecily Millstone was yet another reminder that

no good could come of a relationship with Worth. He'd warned her. Worth was broken and had been for some time. Unable to form a meaningful attachment as evidenced by his broken betrothal to Cecily Millstone. Aurora was sure there were others, but she didn't need to know more. The dowager had done Aurora a great kindness in relaying such a cautionary tale.

"Lady Aurora," Healey said softly, taking her hand. "I think you know that I hold you in great affection and esteem."

Aurora nodded. She'd assumed as much. Counted on it. She turned her face up to his, the perfect position for a kiss. They were far enough from the other couples lingering about that no one would witness if she pressed her lips to Healey's. Aurora had learned the sort of pleasure that could be derived from only a kiss. Or a touch.

And she wasn't going to wed Healey or fall in love with him if they didn't find pleasure together. That had been the entire reason she'd approached Worth.

Not entirely.

A disgusted sound came from her.

"Lady Aurora? Are you unwell? Should I take you back inside."

"You should kiss me, Mr. Healey." She paused. *"Thomas.* You should kiss me, Thomas."

He cleared his throat at the use of his Christian name. "Lady Aurora—"

"Just Aurora, Thomas. We are quite alone. No one will overhear." She took hold of the lapels of his coat and pulled him in her direction. "Put your mouth on mine and kiss me. I insist."

Good lord. She hadn't thought it would prove so difficult.

Healey sucked in a breath, taken aback by her words, but Aurora saw a gleam of desire flickering in his dark eyes. She'd been right. He was hiding a passionate nature behind all that starch. This was better than she'd hoped.

"If you wish, my lady."

"I do. Definitely." Aurora stood on tiptoe.

Healey turned her just so, his lips warm. So were his fingers as he lightly touched her chin. Breath soft and minty, and—

Absolutely nothing.

No humming of her skin. No flutter between her breasts. Her nipples didn't harden to peaks. Disappointing, but there was a *mild* stirring in her mid-section. But—no rush of wetness between her thighs. Or anything at all in that area.

But this was only the first time she'd kissed Healey. Perhaps if she tried harder. This kiss was far too polite.

Aurora boldly pressed her palms flat against Healy's chest, stretching out her fingers. He was warm and solid. Lord Gilroy had stolen a kiss at the end of her last Season and Aurora could feel the ridge of some contraption he wore to rein in his less than manly form. Healey, she was relieved to find, seemed muscular and fit beneath his coat.

"I'm not made of glass, Thomas." Her voice sounded throaty. Seductive. Aurora slid her hands up to his shoulders. "I won't break."

Worth hadn't never considered her fragile. Grabbing her by the throat and kissing her against the bookshelf at Tate's. How Aurora would arch and writhe on his lap while his fingers dug into the flesh of her hips.

"Lady Aurora." Healey attempted to pull away from her.

Aurora grabbed the edges of his coat and held tight, pressing her mouth to his once more.

That languid sensation was certain to fill her bones if he kissed her longer. At any moment, Aurora would be intoxicated, her skin prickling deliciously.

The only thing she felt was a moth landing in her hair.

Aurora opened her mouth beneath his, brazenly trailing the tip of her tongue along Healey's bottom lip. She nipped at his mouth, begging to feel something.

Healey's entire body trembled. A gasp came from him at her boldness. He did not grind his hips against hers.

Drat.

"Well," an annoyed hiss came from behind Aurora. "I hope I'm not interrupting."

CHAPTER TWENTY-THREE

*E*NOUGH OF THIS *nonsense.*

Watching Aurora dance with Healey while that tedious idiot pretended not to stare at her bosom had been one thing, but witnessing her attempts to seduce Kenebruke's nephew was quite another. Charles wasn't sure whether to laugh at the play being enacted before him or toss Healey into the nearest shrub.

Did she want to end up wed to that nitwit?

I don't want her to marry Healey.

Admitting a problem was the first step toward solving it, wise words from the late Viscount Worthington before he'd stooped so low as to tup the woman his son was intent on marrying. The only other person to know of his father's poor decision making was Charles's brother. He'd never even told Drew.

"Mr. Worthington." Healey immediately stepped back from Aurora, leaving one arm to hover possessively near her waist. A silent claim on Aurora. Healey's features ruffled between annoyance and outright challenge at Charles.

Twit.

"My apologies," Charles said smoothly, ignoring Aurora's furious look. "But I've just come about Lord Kenebruke. You may want to have a word with him, Mr. Healey."

Chasing Aurora when he wasn't supposed to and having his thoughts invaded by images of Cecily had put Charles in a mood. Following the pair to the terrace, Charles had made the unfortunate decision to step inside a small parlor hoping for a glass of brandy to help smooth over his emotions. Champagne wasn't working. And Travers was a well-known sot. He had bottles stashed all over his house.

But instead of a finely stocked sideboard, he had been greeted by—*Good lord.* As jaded as Charles was, he had difficulty finding the right words.

"A delicate situation has come about," he finally said to Healey.

Aurora narrowed her eyes at him.

He glared back at her.

"This again, Worthington?" Healey shook his head as if Charles was merely a gnat that continuously annoyed him. Couldn't Aurora see what a pompous idiot he was?

"Have you upset Lord Kenebruke once more with claims of increasing his wealth with your tales of profitable investments?" A cutting laugh sounded. "How dare you take advantage of an elderly gentleman only recovering from his illness." Healey's palm landed at the base of Aurora's spine.

His head would explode if Healey did not step away from Aurora.

"I am handling my uncle's business, Mr. Worthington. I alone am in charge of his affairs." Healey puffed out his chest. "I don't care for the proposition you've put forth. I've reviewed the papers thoroughly and found your investment advice unsound."

So Kenebruke hadn't bothered to tell Healey that the papers had already been signed. He was completely unaware that Kenebruke, Charles, and Drew were now partners in a string of textile mills. Healey had pushed him in the ballroom out of pure dislike.

"That's unfortunate," Charles mused. His temples ached from listening to Healey prance about like that rooster Drew kept at Blackbird Heath.

"My uncle has been quite ill. Your persistence is not helping him heal."

Prig. "Well, Lord Kenebruke did appear to be in pain a few moments ago." The good sort. But Charles kept that to himself.

Healey took a step in the direction of the terrace doors, brows drawn together in concern. "Has he fallen? Or had a fit of some sort?"

"I suppose you might say that." Charles nodded. "He *is* lying down."

"How thoughtful of you, Mr. Worthington, to come all the way out here to find Mr. Healey and inform him of the situation."

Aurora's eyes drew into slits. Not once since Charles arrived had she even attempted to pretend mortification over tossing herself at Healey.

My God. Couldn't she at least pretend?

"I thought Mr. Healey might wish to know," he shot back, watching the spate of conflicting emotions across Healey's face as he tried to determine what to do. Should he drag Aurora inside with him, make a polite excuse, and leave her with the dowager or sprint directly to Kenebruke?

Choices. Choices.

"I'll escort Lady Aurora back inside to Miss Maplehurst," Healey finally said.

"That will be difficult. I fear Miss Maplehurst is otherwise occupied." Charles leaned back and clasped his arms.

Healey's brows disappeared into his hairline. His mouth popped open in horror before snapping shut. "If you'll excuse me, Lady Aurora," he sputtered. "Given my uncle's health, I must see to him immediately."

"I think he's recovered quite well," Charles said blandly.

"Your implications are vulgar," Healey ground out. His left hand curled into a fist.

"That won't do, Healey. You don't want to cause a scene by punching me, do you? There are at least a dozen couples on the terrace. What a scene you'd cause. I wouldn't advise it."

"Always so glib, aren't you Worthington? So smug and full of yourself."

"It's a gift."

A derisive snort came from Aurora.

"Lady Aurora, my apologies, but I need to—"

"Mr. Worthington will see me back inside." Aurora's plump lips were lifted in a brittle smile. "As you know, he's a friend of the family. I've known him since I was a child. Mr. Worthington is like a brother to me."

Touché, Aurora.

"I'll find you once I've seen to my uncle." A look of pure loathing was directed at Charles.

"The small parlor down the hall to the left," he said, as Healey stalked past him. "Can't miss it. The most terrible color of green I've ever seen. Like mashed peas."

Once Healey marched across the terrace and was firmly back inside, Aurora spun on him. "What is wrong with you, Worth?"

"I suppose I'm still addled. Momentarily blinded by what I witnessed. Miss Maplehurst is wearing a red petticoat. Red. At her age." He pushed up from the wall.

"You should not have sent Healey to his uncle."

"I could have pushed him off the terrace and into some shrubbery." Charles took her elbow and moved Aurora further into the shadow and away from any curious glances. The edges of her skirts brushed seductively against his legs and warm honeysuckle filled his nostrils. He was jealous and somewhat aroused. A terrible combination.

Aurora jerked her arm out of his fingers. "Aunt Lottie and Lord Kenebruke—have formed an attachment."

"I'll say."

Aurora kicked him.

"Or rather, they've had an attachment for decades. Long lost lovers, so to speak. Now their reunion will be spoiled. Because of you."

"Are you more upset about the untimely interruption for Miss Maplehurst's sake or your own?"

Aurora shook her head at him. "Just go away, Worth. You

had no right to—burst upon us."

"Are you going to kick me again? Swat me? Or throw a punch?" She looked distraught, furious, and entirely beautiful.

"I'm considering." Aurora straightened her shoulders and looked up at him. She had the stance of someone who knows well how to throw a punch. Unsurprising given she was a Sinclair. Brawlers. The lot of them.

"As it happens, I interrupted your attempted seduction of Healey for your own good. Have you no sense of discretion? Unless you're planning on being compromised and wed within a month, you should not be caught climbing all over Healey like some lascivious vine."

The lines of her mouth drew tight. "Maybe that is what I wish, to be compromised by Mr. Healey. *He* would make a fine husband."

The point being Charles would not. That made him angrier. Never mind that he'd spoken of never wanting to wed dozens of times while visiting Emerson House and decried his viability as a husband.

"He might. But I thought you wanted to wed for love," he said ignoring the terrible ripping sensation in his chest.

"Why do you think I would allow Healey to compromise me if not for love?" Aurora looked away, not answering his question.

"You don't love him."

"Do I not?"

An emotion far worse than jealousy mixed with the tearing of his heart. He should have brought the bottle of brandy with him. But at the sight of those two bodies writhing about on the settee—well Charles was ashamed to admit he'd been shocked senseless especially after recognizing Miss Maplehurst. He'd dropped the decanter he'd only just picked up, spilling brandy all over the carpet.

"Healey is a staid, priggish man you'd tire of in a fortnight," Charles stated firmly.

"You don't know me as well as you suppose." She tilted her

chin. "I *adore* Mr. Healey because he is everything you are not."

As it turned out, Aurora did know how to punch. Those words hit Charles square in the chest. She couldn't possibly know that Cecily had once uttered the exact words, merely swapping Healey for "your father." At the time, she'd been half-naked and draped over the desk in his father's study while Viscount Worthington stammered and attempted to explain the situation.

Their betrayal had gutted him, as if someone had taken a sword and just sliced Charles in half.

Charles grabbed Aurora roughly around the waist, spinning her until her back lay flat against the wall of the Travers' house. Madness possessed him as he pinned her to the stone. Taking her wrists with one hand, Charles pinned her hands above her head.

"Let go of me."

"I don't think I can." Then his mouth fell on Aurora's, hard and angry, savagely stealing her breath. Claiming her mouth as he should already have claimed her.

Aurora sighed. Didn't struggle. Her lush form melted into Charles with a whimper. Every generous curve softening beneath him. Mouth opening without hesitation, Aurora gave him permission to explore the warmth behind her lips, tongue twisting sensually around his own.

Charles felt Aurora, the marvelous sensation of her, steal across his skin and sink into his soul. There was nothing but each other, no sound but their own breathing and the strain to meld their bodies closer.

Not even with Cecily had Charles felt such desperation.

Hand roving over her bosom, his forefinger dipped below the neckline, teasing about until discovering the edge of one pert nipple. The tip of his finger danced along the tiny peak while Charles nipped at the edge of her mouth.

"If this was in *The Bloom of the Rose*," she murmured, back arching, "I don't recall it."

Desire for Aurora, and only her, zinged across his skin like tiny bolts of lightning. Hand ruffling beneath her skirts, Charles trailed his finger up one silk clad leg to the apex of her thighs, cursing the mounds of lace and petticoats separating them.

Aurora moaned softly, lifting her leg around his hip. "Worth."

Charles peered down at her lovely face watching the pleasure light her features at his touch. The truth shone from her eyes. The same truth his heart beat out.

What they really were to each other.

The air stilled in his lungs, unable to take the smallest of breaths.

"It's shameful. You barely touch me, and I am undone," she whispered, a sob catching in her throat. "I can't even claim to be wanton because I don't want anyone else." Aurora sounded so bereft. So incredibly pained.

"Because it's me," he pressed a kiss to her temple. "And—" *It is you.*

Laughter sounded on the terrace, along with the rustling of silk. A throaty, seductive sound. Far too familiar. Charles knew without seeing her who stalked about. Probably looking for him. Lady Bryant would take great pleasure in presenting Aurora as a harlot to anyone who would listen.

And *everyone* would listen.

Aurora could not be found in the shadows with the rakish Charles Worthington, family friend or not. Not with Lady Longwood and her barely restrained desire to declare every Sinclair female a trollop. Charles could not allow that gossip spewing bitch to shame and destroy his brave, beautiful Aurora who had cried over cabbages.

"Hush, Lady Bryant is on the terrace."

"It has always been you, Worth," Aurora hissed at him, seemingly not to care that Lady Bryant was about to declare her a harlot in front of everyone in attendance at the Travers' ball. A push came from the slender hands pressed into his coat. "Even before I found you in the maze. Always. And I don't *want* it to be. Not any longer."

"Aurora," Charles tried to keep his voice even. She couldn't possibly mean that, not now, when he'd finally realized. Decided. "Listen to me," he breathed in the scent of her skin. "You can rail at me later. Curse at me. Hit me with another bowl. But Lady Bryant *cannot* see us together. I'm going to distract her so you won't be noticed. Stay here for a few moments and then go back inside."

"Lady Bryant." There was so much bitterness lacing her words. "Were you aware she is Lady Longwood's cousin when you chased her through the maze? Or saw her...after?"

"After? I haven't seen Lady Bryant—"

"You realize," she interrupted, "what that horrid woman has done to my family, don't you?" Aurora bristled with anger. "She sent us to *Dunnings*. How could you, Worth? Or did your pursuit of pleasure leave you no regard for any of us?"

"Yes. I mean no." Charles looked toward the terrace once more. Lady Bryant was headed in their direction, a purposeful glint in her eyes. "I'm trying to protect you." He took Aurora's arm. "We can discuss all of this tomorrow. Please."

"Protecting me? Ha!" Aurora shook him off. "Or yourself? Don't worry, even if half of the Travers' ball saw us together, I wouldn't ask you to be honorable." She leaned toward him, but stayed just out of reach. "I *know* about Cecily Millstone. What you did to her. I should have listened when you warned me away."

"You've no idea what you're talking about." Charles retreated from Aurora. "You don't know what happened."

"I can guess, Worth." Aurora pierced him with a scathing look. "And I don't want to end up like Cecily. Ruined and discarded so that you can continue your existence debauching every female that comes within arm's length. You will toy with me until I am no longer amusing."

"That isn't—" His eyes fluttered shut for a moment.

Aurora believed the worst of him. Wasn't that what Charles had wanted? To push Aurora so far away that she would never come back?

"Get out of my way."

"But by all means." Charles opened his eyes, careful to regard her with nothing but bored politeness, a far cry from their passion of moments ago. "Don't let me keep you further, Lady Aurora." His tone was chilly, like a pond covered in ice.

She stepped around him.

"Do you know the location of the parlor where your chaperone is tupping Kenebruke?" he snarled at her back. "Two doors down on the left."

CHAPTER TWENTY-FOUR

AURORA SWALLOWED, BUT nothing forced down the absolute sound of desolation threatening to crawl up her throat. Even more reason to get as far away from Worth as possible. Even now she wanted to run back to him.

Marching back toward the terrace doors, Aurora straightened her shoulders. Worth would never allow himself to love and Aurora—well, she must absolutely have love. She had no choice. And Healey? Well, there had been a tiny, miniscule kernel of arousal. Little more than a spark which had immediately sputtered out at Worth's interruption.

Her body, her heart, recognized Charles Worthington in an instant, flaming to life in seconds.

Damn him.

Aurora halted, heels sliding across the stone of the terrace, trying to still the rapid beating of her heart.

The doors, which would take her back inside, loomed large before her. It would be best if Aurora didn't seek out Aunt Lottie. Mr. Healy had likely already barged into the parlor and created a scene. She would go directly to the dowager duchess and request that she be allowed to return home. Immediately.

Worth could *rot* for all Aurora cared.

Damn him.

A sob threatened to escape, and she savagely beat it back. Now was not the time to go about weeping, especially over a man such as Worth.

"Oh dear, a lover's quarrel?" A satisfied voice drawled.

Aurora stopped once more just short of reaching the safety of the house.

Can this evening become any more intolerable?

"I am sorry Worthington felt the need to trifle with you." Lady Bryant came forward with a pout, her sympathy as false as the rest of her. The overly strong scent of her perfume assailed the nostrils, like a pile of rotting lilies.

"Excuse me, my lady." Aurora tried to move around her.

Lady Bryant stepped closer, blocking Aurora's way inside. "Worthington is drawn to innocence. Or at least the ruining of it. I had thought he'd be far more discreet; however, it isn't *his* reputation at stake, is it, Lady Aurora?"

She should have heeded Worth's earlier warning but the Sinclair temper had gotten the best of her. It hurt so bloody much to love the wrong person. A man who could *never* love her back because he wasn't capable. Or worse, just didn't want to.

"Worth is drawn to innocence?" She gave Lady Bryant a confused look and stood her ground when she should have been running away from this vile woman. "Surely yours has been gone for decades, my lady." Aurora blinked. "So what was his interest in you?"

Lady Bryant's grew ugly. A stain of red dotted her cheeks. "He'll *never* wed you. Ruination or not. Everyone knows what Worthington is like, except you, it seems."

Aurora wanted to slap the smirk right off Lady Bryant's crimson lips. But her foolishness wouldn't only harm her, but the entire family. Jordan had worked so hard to reclaim his place in society. Malcolm had a thriving business with ties to Lord Curchon. And Drew. He'd worked so hard to create something with Worth. Aurora had put it all at risk because of her foolishness over a man she couldn't possibly have.

"Charles Worthington isn't the type to marry, though I'm sure you'd done everything in your power to get him to ruin you.

You'll be much better off with Mr. Healey. He's much more likely to fall for your pathetic attempts at seduction. Isn't that what your sister did to gain herself the Duke of Ware? Seems to be what all the Sinclair women do to wed men who are far, far, above their station. Behave like trollops."

A furious puff of air came from her lips. If Aurora's reputation was to be ruined by this horrid woman and Lady Longwood, so be it. She was tired of restraining her behavior with corsets and modesty. Exhausted by trying to be someone she was not. Tamsin would be terribly disappointed, but Aurora no longer cared.

"Sour. Worse than vinegar. Spoiled with rot."

"I beg your pardon." Lady Bryant stepped back.

"You, Lady Bryant. Like a berry which has not been allowed to ripen properly before being picked, though in your case, you have stayed on the vine much longer than necessary. Dangling about, waiting, and hoping someone will harvest you before you become," she leaned in, "shriveled and dry. Tasting of bitterness more than anything else. Speaking of women who wed far above themselves. I've made the acquaintance of Lord Bryant."

Lady Bryant gasped. "You—"

"Trollop? Lightskirt? *Deadly Sin*? Call me what you wish. I no longer care." Aurora matched Lady Bryant's ugly stare with one of her own. "Nothing could be worse than what the gossips whisper about *you*, my lady." Aurora tried to nudge past the blustering woman. A hum was coming from just inside the doors. As if someone had knocked over a bloody nest of wasps.

It appeared Kenebruke and Aunt Lottie had been discovered, and scandal had erupted.

"You're nothing but a baseborn harlot," Lady Bryant sputtered.

"Good grief. I am?" Aurora snorted. "Harlot. Is that the best you can come up with? No wonder you were at Tate's. Your vocabulary belies your own origins," she tossed at Lady Bryant as she strode through the doors, pushing through the crowd of Lady

Travers's guests. Peeking behind a portly man, Aurora caught sight of the parlor, which was now empty.

Out of the corner of her eye, she caught a glimpse of Lady Bryant, her head bent to that of Lady Longwood, who must have been on the terrace the entire time. The pair discreetly stopped nearly everyone returning inside, whispered in their ears with a nod in Aurora's direction.

Oh dear.

Well at least society need wait no longer. Aurora Sinclair had finally showed the wanton behavior she'd inherited from her mother. Lady Longwood must be beside herself with glee. Unfortunately, spoiling Aurora's reputation wasn't likely to earn Lady Longwood any of the coin she needed to stave off her impending poverty.

What a satisfying thought.

Aurora pressed a hand to her midsection. She didn't want to be the next Cecily Millstone, in love with Worth, ruined by him, and then discarded like a sack of spoiled vegetables.

Making her way down the hall and through the ballroom, Aurora skidded to a halt several paces from the dowager and slowed her steps as she'd been taught.

More ladylike nonsense.

"Lady Aurora." The dowager duchess was seated in a cushioned chair, exactly where Aurora had left her. "There has been an incident." She nodded for Aurora to come to her side. "Stop attempting to smooth your skirts. Remain calm."

"Yes, Your Grace."

The dowager duchess took her hand as Aurora waited for the harsh reprimand she sensed between the older woman's pursed lips. Lady Bryant and Lady Longwood had not yet returned to the ballroom to spread their tale, but possibly another guest had seen Worth trap Aurora in the shadows and witnessed their kiss.

I was writhing against him.

Heat stung her cheeks.

"The entire ballroom is watching," the dowager duchess

whispered in an imperious tone. "Every sniveling vile gossip that lives in London. And there are many. Take a deep breath and count to ten before exhaling. Straighten your spine as if a poker has been placed inside." She didn't spare a glance at Aurora, but kept her eyes firmly fixed forward. "Any request to leave will be denied."

"Yes, Your Grace." Aurora inhaled, slowing the release of her breath. "I apologize if I—"

"I blame myself," the dowager duchess said before Aurora could finish.

"You do?" She looked askance at the older woman.

"Yes, of course. I'm the one that knew where Kenebruke had gotten off to. Earlier, I overheard a servant say in passing that an older gentleman whose leg pained him had been placed in what they called 'the ugly parlor.' Having been invited to every ball Lady Travers has ever hosted, I was aware of where Kenebruke had been sent. She sends everyone to that parlor as I may have mentioned." The dowager duchess rolled her eyes. "Heaven knows why. At any rate, the servant further relayed that he asked for a brandy. But that isn't important." A sigh left her. "Now Charlotte has caused a scandal, though at her age I suppose it is to be applauded rather than derided. She has never learned to be discreet. A failing of hers. Doubtless she'll become a countess. Nevertheless, we must remain stoic."

"Yes, Your Grace." Aurora's own transgressions had not been noted.

Yet.

"Your Mr. Healey discovered Kenebruke and Charlotte in a— situation. I believe it was his cry of horror, as if he'd been stuck with a rapier, that summoned nearly every other guest at this ball to the parlor." She raised a brow. "Didn't Mr. Healey escort you outside for a breath of air? Which I would not have approved."

"Yes, Your Grace. Mr. Healey did escort me out. The smell of the gardens is quite lovely. The cooler air refreshing after a dance. The terrace was crowded." Aurora attempted to smooth over any perceived impropriety and clasped her hands. Not that it would do any good in the long run. "However, he felt compelled to check on Lord Kenebruke."

A derisive sound came from the dowager. "I'm sure he now regrets the decision. Rather impolite to leave you alone instead of escorting you back to me. Also, it came to my attention that Mr. Worthington was not in the ballroom. I assume he was playing cards, which he typically indulges in during events such as these. I believe that is how he and your brother became friends."

"Indeed, it is, Your Grace."

"Have you been compromised, Aurora?" The dowager looked straight ahead at the couples dancing before them.

"No, Your Grace." But she had wanted to be. Her leg had been wrapped around Worth's hip. Had he lifted her skirts, Aurora would not have stopped him. No matter her anger, resolve or the words she'd said to Worth, it would never be Healey Aurora wanted. Pointless to deny it. She should be honest with herself if no one else. "I have heeded your advice on such matters."

"So your virtue is intact, but not your innocence, I'll warrant."

Aurora's gasp at her bluntness was quickly covered up by a cough. Best not to answer.

"I will assume, since that mincing nitwit Lady Bryant has just entered the ballroom with that overdone feral pigeon, Lady Longwood, in tow, that you might have seen them in passing as you strolled about with Mr. Healey."

"I did, Your Grace." Aurora clasped her hands tighter. "I believe I compared Lady Bryant to a berry that has been left on the vine to wither, deemed unfit to be picked."

A soft chuckle came from the older woman. "And?"

"There is a strong possibility that Mr. Worthington has not been playing cards."

A huff from the dowager duchess, but no scathing condemnation.

"Very well, Aurora. Tilt up your chin and look down your nose at the lot of them as I've taught you. *We* do not tolerate such talk from lesser mortals, not even when it may be about us. Now, as to the matter of Cecily Millstone," the dowager duchess cleared her throat. "That event should be discussed further. Not with me, mind you. But those with a different view of the situation."

"Yes, Your Grace." Aurora reached down and took the older woman's fingers, squeezing gently. There was a great deal of reassurance to be found with the Dowager Duchess of Ware. "I would like to say, Your Grace, that I bear you a great deal of affection."

"As you should." A smile tried to make itself known on her taut lips. "Maudlin, Aurora. You are becoming oversentimental for a young lady. You must learn to contain such an emotion while in society." But she squeezed Aurora's fingers back. "An important lesson that I insist you learn." Another huff as Lady Longwood strolled deliberately to a group of society matrons across the ballroom. "One hour and we may leave. Stare the feral pigeon down. She won't dare to attack."

"Yes, Your Grace. I will endeavor to do so."

Lady Longwood stalked back and forth, horrid yellow feathers bobbing about in her hair, all pointing in Aurora's direction. Malice had contorted her already sharp features until they were almost unrecognizable. Lady Bryant's lips moved in tandem, pausing to whisper behind her fan and not so discreetly gesture in Aurora's direction.

Aurora didn't flinch. Nor blink. Refused to back down.

She carefully sorted through every horrible thing Lady Longwood had done or said about the Sinclair family. The sobbing of Mama at being banished to Dunnings to die there. Bentley doing his best to starve Aurora and her siblings.

Lifting her chin higher, she said, "Perhaps more a mad hen, Your Grace."

"I can see it," the dowager duchess intoned. "Straighten your shoulders."

An hour later, after three more dances from gentlemen who obviously hadn't yet heard the gossip Lady Longwood was busy spreading, and two glasses of overly sweet lemonade, the dowager duchess finally deemed they could depart.

The guests in the ballroom were far too busy being amused over the news that Miss Charlotte Maplehurst, elderly chaperone, and Lord Kenebruke had been found in a compromising situation to spend much time on Aurora.

But that was likely only due to the commanding presence of the Dowager Duchess of Ware at her side.

Lord Kenebruke had left some time ago with Miss Maplehurst, according to the dowager duchess's footman, who assisted them into their waiting carriage. Mr. Healey was forced to take a hack or find another way home. Someone must have taken pity on him, for Kenebruke's nephew was nowhere to be found.

Aurora fell back gratefully against the fine leather seats with a sigh.

"Kenebruke," said the dowager duchess said as the carriage began to roll, "will not be pleased by the scene Mr. Healey caused. One does not dare to chastise an earl in such a public manner nor dare to disparage the company he keeps. Kenebruke's nephew has overstepped."

Mr. Healey had indeed. "Do you know Lord Kenebruke well, Your Grace?"

"He is a close acquaintance of Lord Curchon and has been for years. I was at the ball when Kenebruke's betrothal was announced. My brother and I were both in attendance. Coincidentally, that ball was Kenebruke's first meeting with Charlotte Maplehurst. I do not know the particulars of their history together, but I saw the earl's face when he first cast eyes on her." The dowager looked at the passing scenery outside. "Identical to Kenebruke's gaze tonight. I believe—he has always loved her. Curchon claimed he did. I'm not sure what caused their recent falling out after so long apart, but I suspect Mr. Healey stuck his nose into his uncle's affairs. So—I sent Charlotte to him."

Aurora digested the information. She opened her mouth to ask more, but the dowager duchess held up a hand.

"It is Charlotte's story to tell. Not mine."

CHAPTER TWENTY-FIVE

T HE CARRIAGE ROLLED to a stop outside of Emerson House, jostling Aurora from her thoughts on Worth. Aunt Lottie. Kenebruke. Her curiosity wasn't satisfied, which would come as no surprise to anyone. She bid the dowager duchess goodnight and pressed a kiss to the older woman's cheek.

"I'm not sure what I would do without you, Your Grace." Aurora meant every word.

"Bah. Soon, you'll start weeping. Fainting spells will be next. I will tolerate not a whit of any of it, Lady Aurora. You will call on me early next week. The cats miss you, especially Hecate."

Hecate was the newest edition to the dowager duchess's collection of felines. A kitten with black fur and green eyes.

"Yes, Your Grace."

Holly opened the door as she bounded up the step, taking her coat with a nod. "Miss Maplehurst awaits you in the drawing room."

"Thank you, Holly." Aurora smiled at the butler, her mood lighter now that she was once more inside the safety of Emerson House. But dread hovered just over her shoulders. Gossip would soon swirl about the *Deadly Sins*. Her mother's name would once more be bandied about and besmirched.

A fire had been lit in the drawing room to chase the night's chill from the air. Aurora looked up at the smiling portrait of her parents above the mantel, knowing the worst was yet to come.

Aunt Lottie's own little scandal would only whet appetites.

I tried to be a lady. I really did.

"There you are." A glass of brandy was clutched in Aunt Lottie's hand. She didn't look at all like a ruined woman should. The glow was back, lighting her from head to toe. A light blush pinked her cheeks, which frankly, could have been the brandy. "I was afraid that old dragon had kidnapped you."

Aurora rushed to the settee and wrapped her arms around Aunt Lottie. "You don't look the least ashamed."

"I'm not." Aunt Lottie winked at her.

"And I think there is much you should thank Her Grace for. I adore her, as you well know. Haven't you put aside your disagreement over the gown?"

"The gown's name was Roderick Candiment. A terrible name. Some of the girls called him 'Roddy Candy' which was barely polite. We both vied for his attention. Good lord, he was handsome, despite the unfortunate name. But in retrospect possessed little sense and barely discernable wit. We both patronized the same modiste, and the gowns she created were nearly identical. My neckline was cut much more dramatically."

"Her Grace informed me."

"Having both arrived at the same ball, dressed nearly alike, and both pursuing Candiment, you can imagine the gossips were rather gleeful. We dueled over him for the remainder of the evening. I won because I didn't play fair." She shrugged. "I allowed a stolen kiss to sway him to my side."

"Aunt Lottie." Aurora drew her brows together in false shock. "I can't imagine."

"Ha!" She took a sip of the brandy. "But Candiment was insufferable, upon further acquaintance. Had a nasty habit of scratching the end of his nose during a conversation. Or the edge of his ear. Like a twitch. Eventually I ended up a spinster. She became a duchess. A dreadfully unhappy one until recently. She adores you in return. As well as Tamsin. You couldn't have anyone better in your corner, Aurora. Her Grace will protect you as if you were her own." Aunt Lottie paused. "Though she is less tolerant of your antics."

"Are you abdicating your role as chaperone?" Because of Kenebruke. Aurora wasn't surprised, only saddened by the news because she would miss knowing the older woman was right down the hall from her.

"For the time being." Aunt Lottie sat up straighter, her tone becoming somber though her eyes twinkled. "I've been *ruined* by Lord Kenebruke." She stared at Aurora a moment longer, looking mournful before bursting into laughter. "Again. I thought I was well past the age of scandal, image my happiness at finding I was not. I won't be a proper chaperone again until I bring Kenebruke up to snuff and he does the honorable thing." Another peal of laughter escaped her. "I suppose I can take up the reins once more if necessary once I'm a countess."

"He is the man you've always loved," Aurora said softly. "All these years, you still longed for him." Aurora thought of Worth. How was she to endure a lifetime of longing for him?

"Yes." Aunt Lottie brushed at a tear that escaped and was making its way down her cheek. "I didn't know Susanna had died when I saw him at the Berriwell garden party. As you can imagine, I tried to keep my thoughts from him." She thumped her chest. "Because it was so painful. But we saw each other and—though now different on the outside, our hearts remained the same. No matter my silver hair or his. Our wrinkled hands. His leg which pains him."

"What happened?"

"When Kenebruke and I first met, he was so bloody honorable. Dutiful. His father had arranged the match with Susanna. I tempted him. Made him fall in love with me. I daresay I seduced him. I was trying to be noble. After. I knew what his honor meant to him. I convinced him that our relationship was merely a dalliance. That I wished to remain unwed. But that wasn't how I felt at all. And I was too afraid to tell him differently." Her voice faltered. "I had no idea that Kenebruke would have broken off the betrothal for me. That he didn't give a fig for his honor when he faced a lifetime forced into a marriage he didn't want. Had I merely allowed him to speak. Tell me what was in his heart—" She wiped at her cheeks once more. "If only I had told him, Aurora. My entire life would have been different."

Worth had been trying to tell Aurora something tonight, but her anger hadn't allowed it. She'd been so caught up the tale of Cecily and his interruption of the attempted seduction of Mr. Healey, which admittedly *was* pathetic, Aurora hadn't allowed him to speak.

"Regret is a dreadful thing, Aurora. Especially when it stretches on for decades, which mine has done. If I had just gone to him." Swallowing the remainder of her brandy, she wiped at a tear.

"But he's here now." Aurora pressed her cheek to Aunt Lottie's hand.

"And he still wants me. As impossible as that seems. When Mr. Healey burst upon us, Kenebruke laughed at his discomfort. He declared, loudly I might add, that he had compromised me and must do the honorable thing. He wants to ask Emerson for my hand, properly, as if I were still that young, reckless creature he once adored."

"You are to him." Aurora's own eyes filled with tears. She was terribly happy for Aunt Lottie and Lord Kenebruke. What a romantic tale. A love that had stayed true across years of separation.

"He is not pleased with Mr. Healey, Aurora. I will warn you now. As much as he loves the boy, Thomas has overstepped, rather dramatically. I will not relate his comments after Kenebruke made his intentions clear. And he purposefully kept us apart." Aunt Lottie plucked at her skirts. "Healey burned my letters to Kenebruke. *Deliberately*. Didn't inform me that his uncle was ill." She lifted her eyes. "Had I known, I would have gone to Neddie and nursed him myself. He thought I'd abandoned him once more."

Neddie. What a boyish name for the elderly earl.

"Mr. Healey is convinced I wish to marry Neddie for his fortune. Which is ridiculous. He had the audacity to ask if Emerson would be providing a dowry. Can you imagine? At my age? I told him that was not the case. Nor did he need concern himself that I would produce an heir for Kenebruke and usurp his position." She gave a rueful laugh.

"All things considered, Jordan probably would provide you a dowry should you require one." Her brother adored Aunt Lottie. They all did. "He can certainly afford to do so."

"Lovely boy. My Neddie would never allow it."

"When will you be wed?"

"At our age it is best not to wait too long. I'll send a note to Odessa in the morning. Once she and Emerson return from Rivercrest, he and I will be wed. Quietly. I can't have him changing his mind."

"I find that unlikely, Aunt Lottie. I have seen you together."

"Neddie doesn't want us apart any longer. I had to force him back to his own home once he escorted me here." She leaned into Aurora with a wink. "However, I will not do so tomorrow evening."

CHAPTER TWENTY-SIX

AURORA INHALED AND exhaled as the dowager duchess had instructed her, carefully pacing out each breath as Mr. Healey strode into the drawing room. She'd considered refusing to see him after Holly announced he had come to call, but Aurora decided he was owed an explanation when she broke off their courtship. Not only had she realized that no amount of kissing would cause her to fall in love with Healey, but there was also the matter of Aunt Lottie. His treatment of Aurora's chaperone told her everything she needed to know about his character.

Frankly, Mr. Healey would not suit.

"Lady Aurora."

"Mr. Healey."

He awkwardly took a seat across from her. "I should explain my sudden absence at the Travers' ball. My departure was rather sudden given circumstances beyond my control, still, I should have sent word to you."

"I was perfectly fine in the company of the Dowager Duchess of Ware." Aurora wasn't certain why she felt the need to remind Healey of her association with Ware's mother, but she thought it necessary.

"Miss Maplehurst resides here so I am certain you were appraised of the events which occurred after I left the terrace at the Travers' ball. My neglect of you was not intentional. But—as you can imagine, I felt the need to come to my uncle's aid."

Aurora blamed Worth for sending Healey in the direction of the parlor and for angering the younger man with thinly veiled innuendo involving Kenebruke. But even if Worth had said nothing, she sensed that Healey's reaction would have been much the same.

"Was calling Miss Maplehurst an elderly lightskirt and imply-ing her interest in Lord Kenebruke to be merely of a financial nature how you offered assistance?" Aunt Lottie hadn't told Aurora, out of embarrassment, most likely. But the dowager duchess had no such reservation.

The tips of Healey's ears pinked. The features she'd once found so appealing darkened. "I stand by my opinion. I have considered for some time how Lord Emerson could allow her to act as your chaperone."

Aurora inhaled through her nose. Slowly. Counted to ten. "The affection between Miss Maplehurst and Lord Kenebruke stretches back four decades," Aurora murmured. "Their association is not sudden or recent. Nor unexpected. A less scandalous conclusion to their relationship would have come sooner if not for your interference."

"My interference?" Healey sat back in the chair, anger cloud-ing his features. "I sought to protect my uncle from a woman who does not have his best interests at heart. He is frail in both mind and body."

Aurora made a piffing sound.

"Her dubious attentions would have only hasten his demise. You cannot possibly comprehend—"

"You kept them apart," Aurora bit out. "Deliberately. Know-ing how deeply your uncle cared for her, and she him. If he had expired from his illness, he would have done so not knowing of her affection for him, which I assure you, is deep and abiding. Is that assisting your uncle or controlling him? I hadn't thought you capable of such deceit, but now I wonder what other meddling you've done in your uncle's affairs."

Healey glared at her, all pretense of politeness having disappeared during Aurora's tirade. "I should have known that would be your opinion." His tone was laden with accusation. "I had reservations about you from the moment we met, but overlooked each one."

"How kind of you."

"Given who you are—"

"Who I am?" Aurora interrupted. This discussion wasn't going at all as she'd imagined.

"A Sinclair. I have ignored certain aspects of your personality until now, but unless drastic measures are taken to mitigate your future behavior, we cannot wed." He lifted his chin. "As an example, a lady should not throw themselves at a gentleman. You practically begged me to take liberties. Kissing me like some—" He stopped, his lips pulling tight. "It is not the manner of a well-bred lady, nor in a woman who is my wife."

"Well, then it is a good thing I don't intend to be yours." Aurora was so bloody incensed, she stopped short of throwing a pillow at his condescending head. How dare he insult her and her family?

A huff left Healey. He shook his head, unable to fathom Aurora's anger. Pinched the bridge of his nose. Abruptly, he jumped up and proceeded to storm about the drawing room, displaying a sort of quiet rage which made Aurora doubly glad of her decision.

"This is because of Worthington, isn't it." He spun about and skewered her with a look. "I've heard the rumors but didn't want to entertain the thought that you could possibly be involved. I should have known when you kissed me like some strumpet. How long have you been lovers?"

Aurora fell back against the cushions, but immediately straightened. The voice of the dowager duchess echoed in her mind.

Steel your spine. Do not look away. Dare them to offer challenge.

"I think it best you leave, Mr. Healey. It is obvious we do not suit. I think it something we can both agree upon."

"There was so much gossip about you and your family, but

like a fool, I ignored the whispers. I've informed my uncle that I will finally take a grand tour of the Continent. I'll be gone for some time and will leave before this travesty of a wedding between my uncle and that woman—"

"Her name is Charlotte Maplehurst. Or Aunt Lottie. But I'm not sure if she'll welcome you addressing her as such."

He glared at her. "Have you nothing more to say, Lady Aurora?"

"I wish you a pleasant journey." Aurora was, in fact, vastly relieved. She needn't worry over running into Healey at Tate's again. Or seeing him at Aunt Lottie's wedding to Kenebruke.

Mr. Healey took a step back. "I was willing to take you, no matter the talk."

He *was* a condescending prig. No wonder Worth didn't like him. "How kind of you. Now you need not take me at all."

"When you are shunned by most of society, without hope of making a decent match, remember me and this conversation. Good day, Lady Aurora." Healey stomped out of the drawing room, nearly slamming into Holly, who opened the door for him. The butler growled softly as he escorted Mr. Healey out, shutting the door behind him.

Bless Holly.

Aurora sat, brittle and still, until the heated conversation with Healey faded from her skin. Well, she'd long suspected there was a passionate nature behind the starched cravat, but Aurora had hoped it would be put to more pleasurable pursuits. Mr. Healey would have made a controlling, rigid husband. Eventually he would have come to watch over Aurora's every mood. Her brothers would have detested him, not to mention Ware.

She did not regret refusing Healey, but it was unfortunate they could not part on more amicable terms. But he'd insulted Aunt Lottie and his uncle. Not to mention finally admitting to Aurora what he really thought of the Sinclairs.

Healey thought Worth was her lover.

Well, isn't he?

Aurora stood and went to the sideboard, poured herself a glass of her brother's best Irish whiskey, and sat back down. Taking a sip, she sighed at the warmth spilling over her chest, hoping to dispel the rest of Healey from her mind. She looked up at the portrait of her parents, the affection they had for each other so bloody apparent.

She took a deep, shaky breath.

"I've never been truthful with Worth. I lied about what I felt because I didn't want to risk my heart. But I suppose I have to. The only alternative would be to live with the regret of not telling him. I don't want to emulate Aunt Lottie. Or wait years to find happiness."

Worth might only love her for a time. Never wed her. But at least, Aurora would have had him.

Swallowing the remainder of the whiskey, she set the empty glass on the table.

"I will have no regrets."

CHAPTER TWENTY-SEVEN

C HARLES LOOKED UP at the sky, thinking what a fine day it was outside, despite the darkening of clouds in the distance that foretold a storm was coming. At least the ride here had been pleasant with the carriage top put down, though the journey had taken nearly an hour.

He hopped out of the carriage, instructing his driver he might be gone for some time before Charles made his way over the neatly kept grass to the gate. This visit was long overdue.

A bouquet of violets was neatly wrapped in paper and clutched in his hand. It was the least he could do.

Violets were Cecily's favorite.

While he'd avoided visiting for years, Charles had known by the hollowness inside him after Aurora stormed away at the Travers' ball, that he would need to see Cecily. There were things that needed to be said. Resolved. He'd gone straight home after leaving Aurora on the terrace, furious at her obstinate nature even though it was one of the things he adored about her. He'd tried to speak to her, though Charles hadn't any idea what he really meant to say.

He'd returned home, frustrated, and unsettled. Taking a seat before the fire in his study, Charles had stared into the flames trying to make sense of his life.

Aurora had nearly been ruined on the terrace by him, barely six feet from the other guests lingering about the gardens. At

Tate's, he wanted to take her to the storeroom and tup her against a crate of books. He couldn't stop touching her. Restraint wasn't working. Or avoidance. The sight of her with Healey had driven him mad with jealousy.

Charles *wanted* to ruin Aurora.

And if he did, he would have to wed her. There was the rub.

He needed to come to terms with the idea of marriage, to Aurora specifically. Charles had told himself for so long that he'd never wed, never love again, that the idea had become second nature. He kept attachments to the bare minimum. Never allowing anything but careless affection to bleed through in his affairs. But if he didn't wed Aurora, Charles would lose her, forever.

His progress across the grass halted as a terrible pain tore into his chest.

Charles would spend the rest of his life knowing Aurora spent her nights in another man's bed, unable to touch her ever again. His petty, stupid reasons for not having Aurora seemed ridiculous. Yes, he was older. And had a reputation. Her brothers might beat him, but Charles would take the risk.

Because Aurora loved him.

She was not Cecily. It was unfair for him to continue to judge her on the actions of another woman.

So, that was how he found himself here, about to forgive that bitch, though part of him wanted to hold onto the bitterness for a lifetime. But this conversation was long overdue, as loath as Charles was to admit it.

"There you are," he said, finally finding Cecily near a bench beneath a large oak tree. Ignoring the bench, Charles instead folded his long legs and sat down in the grass. Taking a flask out of his coat, he tipped it to her, shrugged, and then took a swallow of brandy before speaking.

"I always suspected you were ambitious, but I'd no idea how much. My father was a lonely man, one who had my mother, the love of his life, which you assuredly were not." He looked away.

"I'm sorry if that stings a bit, Cecily. But we both know it to be true. You flattered his ego, a beautiful young woman who wanted to bed a man who most considered past his prime. Guess you proved them all wrong, didn't you."

Charles shifted on the grass. This was hard. Far more difficult than he'd anticipated. The pain of their betrayal still pained him, though at least now when he thought of it, Charles could still take a breath.

"You aren't the first woman to have fucked a man to gain a title. You won't be the last. So banish any thoughts of originality. My brother James was already wed, so I suppose you realized if you wanted to one day be a viscountess, my father was the choice. Marry him. Give him an heir." A bitter laugh came from him. "James knew, by the way, but I didn't tell him." Another sip of the brandy. "He had guessed what you'd done."

Charles recalled the day he had met Cecily. She was exiting the milliner's on a lovely spring day. He'd been struck dumb by the sight of her. "Did you plan to run into me, Cecily? I've often wondered. Our meeting was so…bloody perfect you must have engineered it. How convenient that you were visiting your aunt, who happened to live within a stone's throw of my father's estate. I don't understand why you bothered with me. Why not go straight to him?" He picked up a small pebble and tossed it at her. "We both know why, don't we? You thought I was the eldest. The heir."

He and Cecily had courted in earnest almost from their first meeting. Within a month, Charles had decided to wed her. They spoke of the future. Of the life they might have. Deciding to introduce her to his father, Charles had brought Cecily home, thrilled to see that James was down from London.

"Do you recall the look you gave me when I introduced you to my brother James? The heir?" He made a bitter, choking sound. "You had already seduced me by then, claiming I took your virtue, though I think we can be honest now. It was already gone." He waved a hand. "You took my cock in your mouth far too quickly to have been unexperienced. No coaxing required. Did you use the same trick on my father? Did Lord Dutton appreciate your enthusiasm?" Charles took another sip of the brandy. "Sorry, that was rather impolite. I didn't come here to fight with you."

Viscount Worthington had still been mourning Charles's mother when Cecily was introduced to the family. He'd buried his wife the year before and didn't plan on taking another, something Cecily probably hadn't realized.

A wave of anger hit Charles thinking of what his father had done. But Cecily could be quite convincing.

"You broke my heart, Cecily. And me. I've been walking around with the wounds you inflicted for years. I think you're what killed my father, or at least the shame of you did. I *loved* you, Cecily. And him. You destroyed it all." A sound came from him. "I swore off romantic attachments forever because I saw you in every woman I've met since."

Except one.

At the sight that greeted him that day in the study, Charles ended his engagement to Cecily immediately, no matter how much she and his father begged his forgiveness. She'd fallen to the ground, naked and weeping. His father horrified and ashamed, trousers still down around his ankles.

"You thought my father would wed you. But he didn't. He never would have. Honestly, Cecily, what were you thinking? That you could be my stepmother?" Another ugly laugh burst out of him.

After, Viscount Worthington informed Cecily he had no desire to wed her. Ever. She came crawling back to Charles with the false assumption he loved her so much, he would completely put aside the fact she'd bedded his father.

Charles had laughed so hard at her attempt to reconcile; he'd fallen out of the chair he'd been sitting in. Of course, he was already foxed and would remain so for several days. Her next attempt, showing up uninvited at his London home, had her being escorted out by Ropely's predecessor.

Charles barely gave her a passing thought.

He was far too busy fucking his way through London, debauching any female within arm's reach. Terribly easy. He was charming, wealthy, and good at cards. Seemed the best way to blot out what Cecily had done. It worked remarkably well.

"How that annoyed you, my refusal to allow you back in my life. So instead, you went about town claiming I'd ruined you and then broke our betrothal. I was labeled a cad for discarding you. The worst sort of gentleman. And I allowed you to because I simply didn't care."

He did not compromise young ladies of good family, because marriage would be the end result, something Charles meant to avoid at all costs. If a lover became clingy or spoke of the future, Charles ended the relationship without a thought. Most importantly, he kept his heart well out of reach, locked away where it could never be found. You cannot have your heart or trust broken if you refuse to give either.

So, Charles didn't.

"I see you've nothing to say for yourself, Cecily. Just as well." He looked up at the sky which had darkened. "I don't wish to be caught in the rain. Oh, nearly forgot. I brought you these as a peace offering."

He took the small bouquet of violets and placed them atop the mound of Cecily's grave. The problem with speaking to the dead was that it was a one-sided conversation. Still, it felt good to say the things which had infected him for so long.

Cecily, Lady Dutton, had died of consumption two years into her marriage to Lord Dutton. The news of her death broke him, though since he'd locked away his heart, the pain was rather muted. She'd written to him. Repeatedly, before she coughed out her life.

Charles burned every letter without reading it.

A year later, Charles forgave his father as he lay on his deathbed. Then he was gone too.

The debauchery that had become his life worsened after that. Until James came to London and forcibly removed Charles from a brothel where he had been enjoying himself for over a week.

"Enough, Charles. They are both gone. Do you wish to join them in your anger?"

Bless James. He was an excellent older brother. Not at all like Drew's prick of a brother, Bentley. Even better, James had ensured that Charles would never have to be a viscount or be motivated to produce an heir. He had a brood of four boys, all of whom Charles loved dearly.

"You see I can love." It was only that he was picky about who he gave his heart to. "Because of the scars, Cecily."

There had been so many women since then. Meaningless affairs which failed to move Charles one way or another. He played a great deal of cards and eventually discovered his ability to glean information from his opponents, small details that seemed meaningless. But those tidbits helped Charles decide where to invest. Not large sums at first. But later. He was good at it. Now, not only investments, but other business dealings and enterprises that would prove fruitful.

He looked down at the weathered stone where Cecily's name was etched along with a pair of dates. Dutton had rewed barely a year later and probably never visited Cecily. That was why Charles had brought her flowers.

Aurora would need to know the truth. Not the rubbish Cecily had spouted off about. He couldn't bear for Aurora to think he'd abandoned Cecily after ruining her.

If he could get her to speak to him again.

Charles had other things he wanted to tell Aurora. To be patient with him because his heart was fragile, and he was terrified. But he was meant to be hers.

After placing the violets, Charles stood. "I cannot allow you or your memory to take Aurora from me, and thus I forgive you, Cecily Millstone. I regret that I could not do so before you came to rest here, but I wasn't able. I hope you understand." A lone tear traveled down his cheek, and he brushed it away. "I loved you. Truly. And I'm sorry I didn't read your letters, because I think I should have."

Charles wandered over to the bench and sat for a long time, sipping at his flask of brandy. He felt lighter, though if anyone happened upon him, they'd think Charles mad, drinking brandy and speaking to a bloody gravestone. Aurora Sinclair was a terrifying prospect, for all the right reasons. But he had to put such fears aside. He wanted Aurora.

"Enjoy the violets, Cecily."

He finally came to his feet and walked back to his carriage just as the first drops of rain hit his shoulders. How best to approach Aurora? Seduction would be his first choice, but given her mood, that might not be best. Apologize, absolutely, for being such a prick most of the time and pushing her away. Court her? Yes. That was likely the only way she'd see that his intentions were completely honorable. The idea made his stomach pitch violently. Not because of Aurora but—

He'd have to go to Emerson and ask permission, and even then, Charles wasn't sure Aurora would accept him. So maybe seduction and then see her brother.

Emerson might simply call Malcolm to shoot him.

Maybe Charles should start with Drew.

He mulled over his options the entirety of the return trip home and still hadn't decided what to do when he left the carriage to jog up the steps.

"Mr. Worthington." Ropely opened the door and took his coat. "You have a visitor."

Charles frowned. There had been no carriage sitting outside. Nor was he expecting anyone. Unless Kenebruke had sent over his solicitor? Which made no sense since the papers were already signed, but maybe he had additional questions. As long as it wasn't that twit Healey.

Tossing his coat at Ropely, Charles walked toward the drawing room.

"Sir—" Ropely tried to stop him.

Charles walked into the room and was immediately assaulted by the scent of honeysuckle and the sight of Aurora seated calmly on the sofa, wrapped in her cloak, *The Bloom of the Rose* open on her lap.

CHAPTER TWENTY-EIGHT

"AURORA."

Worth appeared as if he might faint at the sight of her. She couldn't discern if he was pleased or distressed to find her sitting in his drawing room once more. Not that she gave a fig for his opinion at present. She wasn't leaving. Not until things were resolved between them, no matter what form that took.

"Page forty-two." Aurora held up the book. *The Bloom of the Rose* had been sitting on a side table near the window. There was a bit of jam stuck to one page, as if he'd been eating breakfast one morning and just leafed through pages of sexual acts between bites of toast before putting the book aside.

Worth glanced down at the small leather tome. "What are you doing here?"

"I'm not leaving," she challenged.

"I didn't ask you to."

He'd been outside, somewhere. There was dirt on his boots and grass stains on his trousers, which she perused while the fabric tightened along his thighs.

Goodness. He was happy to see her. "Page forty-two."

Aurora absolutely refused to live with forty years of regret. She didn't even want to experience the feeling for one more minute. Her expectations of Worth were low. Marriage wasn't in her immediate future. Possibly he would only grant her a discreet dalliance. Worth might not love her, but he did hold her in affection. His desire for her was clear.

She glanced down once more at the way his coat had tented above his thighs.

The life of a mildly scandalous spinster with a rakish lover might suit her quite well.

But at the very least, Worth needed to know where Aurora stood. Her emotions would no longer be in question. What he chose to do with the information was another matter, but there would be no more questions.

He *was* capable of love. He'd nearly married Cecily Millstone for goodness' sake, so it wasn't an entirely foreign concept. She'd wanted to ask Aunt Lottie about Cecily, but her former chaperone was too busy making plans to wed Lord Kenebruke. Odessa and Jordan were even now on their way back to London. Drew was coming from Lincolnshire. Malcolm and Alyss were already here, of course. Emerson House would be full to bursting—not as full to bursting as Tamsin, of course; the new Marquess of Sokesby could be born at any minute—but within a day or two, Aurora would be surrounded by her family. This was the only chance to make her case.

"I thought you had learned all you wished," he said softly, eyes glinting a deep blue as he moved toward her. "Dismissed yourself from my tutelage."

"I was mistaken. I fear I'm quite lost without direction. You witnessed me with Healey."

"Don't remind me."

Ah, there was that lovely flash of jealousy. "I am also interested in Chapter fifteen, page fifty."

"Chapter fifteen?"

"Chapter fifteen describes how to properly put the male appendage into a woman's mouth to bring about great pleasure. The male cock."

"I'm aware of the term." Worth drew closer, warming the air around her.

"There are various things I'm to do with my tongue. Suck

upon it like a string of licorice."

Worth's eyes had gone so dark the pupils disappeared. "Licorice? More sucking the ice off a spoon."

"You see? I require guidance." Aurora sniffed the air. "You smell of brandy. Have you been drinking?"

"Have you?" His voice grew thick, sniffing her back. "What is on page forty-two?"

"Deflowering of a virgin." Aurora's hand shook slightly as she lowered the book. "Relieving me of my maidenhead."

"I know what deflowering means, Aurora." He came forward, a strained look on his handsome features. "Do you?"

"I am completely aware of what the outcome of this demonstration will be." She stood, shut her eyes and tossed off the cloak. "I've come prepared."

"Dear God." Worth sucked in a breath. She heard him grab the arm of the chair next to him. "You're naked."

"Observant. I'm pleased to know that given your age, you do not need spectacles."

"My age?" The ragged sound of his breathing filled the air.

"One of the reasons why you—find yourself unsuitable for me. I tend to value the experience you've gained." She sucked in a breath, deciding not to finish her thought. It took a great deal of courage to stand naked before the man she loved, hoping that he wouldn't reject her.

"You're so beautiful, Aurora." There was awe in his words. "I've always thought so. Inside as well as out. Even when nearly taking off my leg at bowls."

"I'm not athletic. I'm not sure why you are surprised."

The drawing room was silent, the only sound her heart roaring in her ears and Worth's steps as he circled, likely examining every inch of her. Aurora wasn't sure, because she was too embarrassed to open her eyes. If he was going to throw her out, Aurora wished he would do so. She'd gather the cloak, her pride, and never bother him again.

"You want me to ruin you." The low purr caressed her ears.

"I do," she said, still not opening her eyes. "Now, either do so or have Ropely toss me out."

The barest touch of his finger traveled along the slope of her collarbone. "You are a brazen thing, Aurora Sinclair."

"Wanton, if you listen to gossip." Aurora opened her eyes. She was feeling rather hopeful.

The warmth of his mouth fell over her neck, breath trailing along her skin to press a kiss at her shoulder. Standing before her, Worth moved to cup one breast, pressing another kiss to the tip of that sensitive peak.

Aurora shivered.

"Are you cold? I'll warm you. Promise." Worth's hand splayed wide, shifting slowly to her stomach before coming to his knees.

"I'm not cold," she whispered.

"I didn't mean to upset you at the Travers' ball." His breath drifted over the hair of her mound and skin of her thighs. "I— behaved poorly, Aurora."

"Yes, you did. But I should not have said—I didn't want it to be you." A sob caught in her throat. "Because it has always been you, Worth. So here I am. I don't want anyone else. I tried to feign interest in every gentleman presented to me since my come out and nothing works. I know you might never—" her voice caught, "return my depth of feeling. But there is something between us, and I'm tired of pretending I haven't longed for you since my first Season. It's only put me out of sorts."

"I find I am also out of sorts." The flick of his tongue traveled along the inside of her thigh. "There are so many wicked things I will do to you." His teeth sank into the soft flesh there.

"That will leave a mark," she bit out as the pain throbbed along her skin, pulsing at that place between her thighs. Aurora tilted her hips forward. This was a lovely distraction.

His mouth fell over the spot, licking gently. "I hope so," he whispered. The press of his thumbs pulled her thighs wider apart. "You smell enticing, Aurora." One hand took hold of her hip.

"Yes, but page forty-two—"

"I'm getting to that, Aurora. These things cannot be rushed." His finger slid into her folds, gently exploring, though he'd touched her there before. Stroking at the small bit of flesh, he teased at it until a guttural sound came from her.

The pad of his tongue flicked out, tracing along the same path his fingers had blazed, drawing out yet another moan. Aurora's fingers threaded through the thick gold of his hair, holding him close to her. "I think," she panted, "that we have already covered this chapter."

"Haven't you ever reread your favorite passages of a book?" The tip of his tongue touched her flesh once more, sliding and teasing. He brought Aurora to the very brink of her pleasure, frightfully easy to do. She wasn't even a decent challenge.

Worth came to his feet, drawing his body up the length of hers. One arm circled Aurora, bringing her close to the warmth of his chest. The other moved between her thighs.

Aurora clutched at his shirt.

He pressed his forehead to hers, eyes on hers, intent, as two of Worth's graceful, beautiful fingers sunk deep inside her.

"Worth."

"I want it to be me. If nothing else, I cannot watch you tossing yourself at the likes of Healey again." His eyes closed and the tip of his nose rubbed against hers. "All of which was unnecessary. You should have allowed me to speak." His fingers stroked while his thumb brushed that tiny bit of flesh in a teasing manner.

"That was rude of me," she panted, heart racing with desire and love for him.

Again, he took Aurora to the very pinnacle as she waited for him to push her over the edge, but instead he only moved her to the settee. Carefully he laid her down, clever fingers moving inside Aurora the entire time. "Please, Worth."

His fingers retracted and a small wail of disappointment came from Aurora.

"Don't bring Ropely to the door." Worth discarded his coat

and tossed it to the floor.

"Shirt next," she insisted. "Then the rest."

"You're a virgin, Aurora. You should be quivering and weeping at your fate. Though given the things I've already done to you, and your own nature, I suppose that isn't possible."

"I will weep if you don't pleasure me, this instant."

Worth undid his cravat, throwing it over the arm of the sofa. "We may need that later," he winked. "I'm not sure if it is covered in *The Bloom of the Rose*, so we might improvise." He pulled off his shirt.

Aurora had seen a bare male chest before. She'd grown up outside of Spittal which boasted brawny sailors who crawled along the docks, sometimes shirtless. Also, she had three brothers. But the sight of Worth…

Arousal snaked up her body.

Worth was all smooth, sculpted muscle, each graceful movement stretching beneath his skin. So beautiful, like a statue crafted by a master artist. No wonder Lady Bryant had nearly wept when he left her. Sleek and golden, like a great cat, with the delicious indentation of bone at his hips, a place Aurora wanted to press her mouth to.

When he doffed his trousers, a gasp came from her.

"Oh."

"Yes, oh." Worth and his cock—that was the name Rose in *The Bloom of the Rose* most often used—pointed directly at her as Worth settled on the settee to hover over her. The tip batted against her mound. "This will change things between us, permanently, Aurora." The teasing was gone from his voice. "You must be sure."

"Well, yes." She looked up at him. "Of course it will change things. I'll no longer be a virgin. You will have ravished me." Aurora gave him a cheeky smile.

Worth's head dipped once more, mouth and tongue suckling at the skin of her breasts, worshipping the taut peaks of her nipples, bringing all that pleasure back but offering no relief. His fingers moved inside her once more, curling and stroking until Aurora thought she might go mad. She grunted in frustration as he withdrew once more. "Teasing me in such a way is—"

"So impatient." He pressed a kiss to her lips. "Spread your thighs further apart."

The press of his cock rubbed against her entrance.

Aurora lifted her hips. "Please, Worth." Her teeth sank into his collarbone.

"Ruination guarantees I'll wed you," he whispered.

"It doesn't have to." She kissed him fiercely. "I won't expect you to be honorable."

"But what if that is what I choose?" He stayed, cock poised at her entrance. "You wish to wed for love." He nipped at her bottom lip. "Do you mean that?"

Worth was asking if she loved him. The rhythm of her heart beat fiercely. For him. Always for him. "What makes you think I wouldn't be?" she breathed.

A smile tugged at his lips as he opened himself to her, reluctantly. But that was Worth. He hid his emotions so well behind a handsome, charming mask.

But Aurora saw everything.

Especially his heart.

That tortured battered thing he'd kept hidden along with the absolute fear of offering it to her. Something had changed in him since the Travers' ball, something he hadn't yet told her about.

She cupped his cheek. "I will be careful with you, Worth. As you are with me."

Worth's eyes stayed on hers as he thrust inside, ripping through what was left of her innocence in an instant. Her muscles fluttered and stretched at the invasion. Aurora had expected the pinch of pain.

Concern for her marred his features.

"I'm well." Her fingers clasped at his hips. "You may continue."

"Aurora," he whispered, and kissed the tip of her nose. "I

think a marriage for love…" He took up a slow, sensual rhythm. "Will suit us both."

"Agreed." Aurora's head fell back, hips moving in unison with his, her mind going still at the thought of the pleasure building inside her.

"I love you," she wrapped her legs around his waist as the waves of bliss began to break across her skin.

A groan left him, her name on his lips, as Worth's pleasure followed her own.

Aurora clasped him tighter.

She would never let go.

CHAPTER TWENTY-NINE

THE VICAR WAS speaking of love. Devotion. How marriage was a bonding of two hearts.

Aurora sniffed. Such beautiful words. A tear rolled down one cheek. She drew in a long breath, counted to ten, and composed herself.

"Don't cry, my love." A warm palm splayed discreetly across the base of her spine, and Aurora drew a relieved breath. She was standing toward the back of the group of family and well-wishers, deliberately, waiting for Worth to appear.

"Did you speak to Jordan?" She whispered, turning only slightly to inspect his handsome features. Not a hair out of place. No bruises or cuts to mar his perfection.

Well, that was good, wasn't it?

Worth had been ushered in to Emerson House well over an hour ago and requested to speak to Lord Emerson. Aurora had wanted him to wait until after Aunt Lottie and Lord Kenebruke's celebration, but the gossip had already started about her and Worth. There were even some outlandish claims Aurora had been seen visiting Mr. Charles Worthington, unescorted.

"I did." His fingers stretched along her back. "Pay attention to the vicar. Aunt Lottie is radiant."

The older woman glowed in her blue dress lined with silver thread, her eyes on no one else but Kenebruke. Adoration that was returned by her groom. Odessa stood beside Aunt Lottie, dabbing at her own tears as Kenebruke solemnly spoke his vows.

Odessa's shoulders shook with a silent sob.

Jordan drew her into the circle of his arms. His chin tilted at an angle, eyes narrowing as he took in Worth and Aurora.

Aurora gave her eldest brother a weak smile.

"The discussion with Jordan went well?" Oh, there it was. A tiny cut and spot of blood on Worth's lip.

"As well as could be expected. Only Drew punched me."

Drew and Malcom were summoned to the study by Holly, shortly after Worth had arrived. The four stayed closeted until just before the vicar's arrival. Her brothers had all filtered into the drawing room, but not Worth, until moments ago.

Aurora kept her eyes on the back of Aunt Lottie's head as her former chaperone repeated her vows to Lord Kenebruke.

"Emerson didn't seem overly surprised by my proposal. Nor Malcolm, though he did mention shooting me. I am only grateful that due to the birth of the Marquess of Sokesby, Ware was not waiting about in some dark corner to trounce me."

"Jordan has heard the gossip."

"Everyone in this house has heard it, Aurora. And most of London. Thankfully, according to Malcolm, Lady Longwood is even now on her way to the country. Her son, Viscount Longwood, has apparently fled England for a time. The details were not made clear to me."

"Probably best you don't know." Aurora thought of what the dowager duchess had inferred at the Travers' ball. "I am only glad she is gone."

A round of applause lit the air as the vicar introduced Lord and Lady Kenebruke. The Sinclairs surrounded the happy couple, offering congratulations. Holly arrived a moment later to announce a wedding feast awaited them in the dining room.

As Hester and Drew passed by, Aurora's brother slammed his shoulder into Worth.

Oh. Dear.

"Drew is a little upset with me at present, but it will pass,"

Worth informed her. "He'll be too busy with Kenebruke's textile mills to stay angry for long, at any rate. He wants us to wed before his return to Lincolnshire."

Aurora nodded. "He's afraid you'll change your mind."

Worth had told her about Cecily and his father. How he'd allowed everyone to think the worst of him because the truth was too painful and humiliating. How becoming a rake had less to do with Worth being a libertine, and more to do with a broken heart. She thought he would tell Drew the truth about Cecily. Eventually.

"I assured Drew I had no intention of breaking our betrothal," Worth said. "Even if all three of your brothers, plus Holly, hadn't threatened me with bodily harm, I am still determined to marry you." The blue of his eyes twinkled down at her. "And not because I'm honorable. Our marriage is for love and nothing else."

The rest of the family filtered into the hall, but Aurora paused, fingers tracing the lapels of his coat. "So, things are settled?"

"Yes. In a manner of speaking. But you aren't allowed to visit me until the vicar pronounces us wed. Emerson doesn't want the gossip to become that much worse. I'll likely be subjected to the dowager duchess as your chaperone until then, given Aunt Lottie will be otherwise occupied."

"A courtship and chaperone are not required," Aurora stated. She'd been hoping to be left alone with Worth when he paid a call. Or if they chose to view the gardens behind Emerson House. "Did you mention such?"

"I believe that is why Drew punched me."

Worth took her arm and escorted Aurora into the dining room, pulled out her chair, and winced before straightening.

"Worth?"

"Emerson packs a punch. The tales of his brawling in taverns was not an exaggeration."

They both looked up to see Jordan watching them from the

head of the table, a smirk on his lips.

"As I said, I am only glad Malcolm didn't shoot me."

"There's still time," Malcolm leaned across the table. "Say the word, Aurora."

"Leave off, Mal." She lowered her voice. "Good lord, you ruined Alyss." Aurora nodded to her sister-in-law. "No offense, Alyss."

"None taken," Alyss replied with a wave.

Aurora took Worth's hand under the table and stroked his fingers. "I'm sorry. I thought my family would be better behaved. I should have known."

There was still Tamsin to contend with, but the dowager duchess had likely suspected Aurora's involvement with Worth since the Travers' ball.

"Don't worry. I'll survive." He promptly placed her palm between his legs before winking at her. "Three weeks at most."

"An eternity," Aurora huffed.

"A toast." Kenebruke held aloft a glass, his gaze on Aunt Lottie. "To my bride, more beautiful now than the day I met her. My dear Charlotte."

The entire table raised their glasses in toast as Aunt Lottie blew a kiss to her groom.

The new couple would reside in Kenebruke's London house until the end of the Season, and then retire to the quiet of Northumberland and the earl's estate for a time. Aurora would miss Aunt Lottie, but at least the older woman would still be in London for a spell.

Aunt Lottie deserved every happiness.

Aurora sat back in her seat, fingers still entwined with Worth's, and observed her family, the love flowing about the table. Dunnings no longer dictated the existence of the Sinclairs. Nor Bentley. Lady Longwood had been vanquished, though a pity it hadn't been by her hand.

"I love you." Worth's lips caressed the edge of her ear.

She smiled back at him. "I know."

EPILOGUE

Rivercrest, one year later

"ARE YOU TRYING to maim me?" Charles danced out of the way of the bowl barreling across the manicured lawn of the Earl of Emerson's estate. "Good god. Try to pay attention."

"How often have I told you," Aurora waddled in his direction, "I am not athletic. And I am overburdened at present."

"She's enormous," Odessa said, walking past Charles. "And barely six months along. Twins, I'll wager."

"Stop staying that," Aurora hissed.

Charles felt lightheaded at the thought of two children at once. If his wife didn't murder him with a poorly thrown bowl, he might just expire from worry over her condition. He'd taken to hovering over her, as embarrassing as that had become. He was likely to be even worse as a father.

Drew found his behavior, given Charles had been an unrepentant rake for so long, hilarious.

Emerson tossed his bowl and scored. He was dreadfully good at this game.

"It could be Alyss, you know." Charles nodded to Malcolm's wife, who was also with child once more. "She's overly large."

"Are you insulting my wife?" Malcolm grinned as he took up his position. "Though, quite honestly…" He peered at Charles. "One of them is bound to have twins. Runs in the family. I suppose three at once isn't out of the question. According to Ware."

The Duke of Ware was barely visible, his large form crawling about the garden collecting specimens while the rest of the family was forced to play a game on the lawn. Charles would have thought it unfair that the duke didn't have to participate, except that yesterday, His Grace had thrown a bowl so hard he'd taken down a small shrub.

"Three?" Charles pinched the bridge of his nose. "Dear God. It could just as well be the duchess."

Tamsin, Duchess of Ware, strolled along the edge of the lawn, observing the proceedings with a glare. She'd been disqualified the day prior from further play and was not at all pleased. Emerson had caught her cheating.

"Excellent point. But Lord Sokesby was so large that I can't imagine," Malcolm shrugged, "how Tamsin would have—room."

He and Charles exchanged a glance before both turned away. Not a topic either wanted to pursue.

"I don't care for this game at all," Aurora announced. "And I'm starving." She walked toward him, face flushed. "Is there anything to eat?"

Charles immediately came to her side and wrapped an arm firmly about her waist.

"I can make it to a chair without assistance." She swatted at him. "No need to hover. You're becoming like Ware." She grunted as he helped her sit.

Aurora was often hungry. Tired. Excessively—*aroused*. Frankly, Charles was a bit exhausted.

He settled her and then pressed a kiss to her temple. Pouring out a lemonade, he handed it to her.

"I should probably take a nap." Aurora smacked her lips, eyes roaming over Charles. "I think you should see me up the stairs to our room. Maybe assist me in a bath."

Aurora, all round and soft, floating about naked in a tub of water with soap bubbles clinging to her, was much more appealing than a game of bowls. Besides, Charles could do with a nap.

He was so lost in his vision of Aurora in the bath, he didn't answer right away.

Aurora pinched him. "I'm bigger than one of Hester's beloved cows." She looked at him, tears glistening in her eyes.

"You are not." He pressed a kiss to her temple, thinking how much he loved Aurora and their life together. If not for her, Charles would have missed out on all of this. Not a game of bowls, of course, but a family. Contentment. Peace the likes he never thought he'd have.

"Come," he lifted her gently, squeezing her backside as she giggled. "Let us get you into a bath."

About the Author

Kathleen Ayers is the bestselling author of steamy Regency and Victorian romance. She's been a hopeful romantic and romance reader since buying Sweet Savage Love at a garage sale when she was fourteen while her mother was busy looking at antique animal planters. She has a weakness for tortured, witty alpha males who can't help falling for intelligent, sassy heroines.

A Texas transplant (from Pennsylvania) Kathleen spends most of her summers attempting to grow tomatoes (a wasted effort) and floating in her backyard pool with her two dogs, husband and son. When not writing she likes to visit her "happy place" (Newport, RI.), wine bars, make homemade pizza on the grill, and perfect her charcuterie board skills. Visit her at www.kathleenayers.com.

Milton Keynes UK
Ingram Content Group UK Ltd.
UKHW021042170524
442867UK00013B/574